THE FRENCH WOMAN

and other stories

by   Nabil Louis

All Rights Reserved

To my Wife and my Daughter

Contents	Page
1. The Sad Tale of Giuseppe Pellaggio	5
2. The French Woman	31
3. Vladimir	65
4. Amos the Parisian	77
5. The Assessor	117
6. My Close Friend	133
7. James and the Little Mermaid	151
8. My Encounter with a Shark	177
9. Max	181
10. In Search of Love	183
11. The Artist	205
12. King Lear of the Steppes	213

THE SAD TALE OF GIUSEPPE PELLAGGIO

I knew Pellaggio since we were very young children at the age of five. His family came to live in the Spanish quarter in Napoli opposite the church Trinita di Spagnoli where we lived. We became inseparable, and I was always welcome at his home whenever we liked to play. I remember his mother, a very beautiful and elegant lady, totally devoted to her family and her home. I did not see his father much as he was mostly away on business. My parents liked Giuseppe and they were always pleased to see me keeping him company, welcoming him into our home. He was an average boy from an average middle class family, and so was I. The only striking thing about him were his sparkling eyes. He was always animated, and so was I, and that was probably the secret that we got on so well. We used to play with train models, colour and paint, and spread coloured beads of various sizes on the carpet to make gigantic shapes. We would laugh, and start running in circles around the models we have made, feeling happy. At the age of seven, we were allowed to go out on our own, and we used to stroll up and down Via Toledo watching the men sitting at little tables laid outside on the pavement in the trattorias tucking into large neapolitan pizzas and washing it down with large gulps of beer in tall glasses. We would recognise the same diners every time and they in turn had got used to our strolling past them. We would walk up Via Toledo all the way to the main central station, and then down again past the side street that takes us back to our homes all the way to Piazza Plebiscito where we would hang around for hours in its vast space. We played around the many columns on either side of the beautiful Roman building, counting them each time and checking that they were of equal numbers on both sides. If we had time, we would make our way to the water front along the promenade and watch the big ships in the port. I have always loved the sea, something that Giuseppe also shared. It was that immense freedom when looking at the limitless water expanse that fascinated us, and it was this freedom that we cherished the most, little that Giuseppe knew at the time that one day he would lose the one thing that he grew to value and seek as indispensable. Walking along the main via we had divided those grand edifices between us, those that belonged to me and those that belonged to Giuseppe. They were of monumental architecture, rich in statues and ornaments at their very top, and among them the university building which fell to me. How I remember Giuseppe's laughter and the happiness that shone in his eyes. And how I long back to those days when he was on top of the world, happy and safe, playing and acting with all the good innocence that the grown up world does not understand and had long forgotten.

I am of Spanish ancestry. My grandparents had settled in Italy a century before and had chosen to live in Napoli. They had only one daughter who married into an Italian family. My father worked as an engineer for the local government. Like their parents they had only one child, me. I was considered handsome by the general standard, and I grew up in a loving family. Our life rotated around my mother, for she brought perfect harmony and instilled in me a wonderful sense of duty and discipline. My father provided the means and my mother presided over our way of life. I always marvelled at her wisdom and her generosity of heart, never wavering from her daily obligations. If everything flowed smoothly it was because of her. When home, my father was happy to let it be and step in the background. When you met my mother you immediately thought she was a serious person, but soon you marvelled at her devotion to her family and her home. It was her world and her life, and like the fish needing water she could not live outside of it. It was her entire being.

Giuseppe came from old Italian stock. His father was a businessman and was away from home most of the time. The family lived in the ground floor apartment below us. Our apartment on the first floor with a large balcony looked modest by comparison to theirs. Mrs Pellaggio was also a devoted mother and housewife. You could glimpse her exquisite taste in the way she furnished her home. I can still remember the way she dressed, and the elegant way with which she talked and walked. She took great pride in dressing her son smartly. In those days I could be at times coarse in my behaviour, but Mrs Pellaggio understood boys ways and was keen that I behaved impeccably in the same way as her son was taught to act and behave. I was so glad of those interventions and I accepted them whole heartedly and without hesitation or rancour. If I owe much to my present elegance and refinement it is to Mrs Pellaggio.

Giuseppe and I went to the same primary school in Napoli and later to the same secondary school. I was keen on mathematics but Giuseppe deep at heart remained a big child, attracted by play, and he had a fascination for ceremonies and outward displays. Neither of us pursued any further studies after secondary school, and we were in a hurry, each in his own way, to leave home and forge a career in the world. With my father's intercession I joined an accountancy firm in Sorrento, an hour's journey by train from Napoli. I rented a small flat in the town not far from the office, and was happy at work. Giuseppe decided to enter the Army. I remember having a long conversation with him soon after making his decision one weekend when I was back in Napoli to see my parents, as I did not think he was the right character for it, but he assured me that that was what he wanted to do and that he felt he would do well as an officer. In fact he appeared quite relaxed about it. We parted company, wishing each other success and good fortune.

My name is Pietro. At my birth my mother wanted to name me Pedro but my father insisted it should be the Italian version. As I have said, I settled well in Sorrento and I was enjoying the work that I was doing and the tasks assigned to me tremendously. I enjoyed living in this beautiful town overlooking the sea from a cliff, and every evening in the summer I went down to Piazza Tasso, the central hub of the town, and stood at the parapet looking out to the azure blue sea in the distance and studying the small ferries that took people to and from Capri. I thought often of Giuseppe and how he was getting on in the Italian Army. We kept in touch via letters, for we did not have mobile phones or the Internet in those days. He was upbeat in his letters and I learnt that he was stationed in the province of Calabria. He did not mind the heat, but he missed being near the sea. He had passed his initial training and was now in the rank of secondary lieutenant.

One day I had a wonderful surprise. I came back to my flat after work to be informed by the concierge that my friend Giuseppe was in town and will be waiting for me in the Franciscan church which is only a short walk from Piazza Tasso. I hurried there and I found him sitting in one of the benches right at the front in meditation. We embraced and looked at each other in amazement. He had not changed in his outward appearance, but there was a note of seriousness and maturity about him. He was still as bubbly as ever but I could detect something new in him, for he looked somewhat weighed down. I put it down as the sign that he had now moved into the real world of grown-ups, where the innocent fun stopped and where the responsibilities took over. I took him to a little gem of a restaurant tucked away in one of the little streets off Tasso. He ordered sea food risotto and I had linguine with lobster over a bottle of red Barolo. Giuseppe was able to relax and open his heart.

He said to me " Pietro, I feel bewildered and at times quite overwhelmed. As much as I looked forward to an independent life, I did not know how much sheltered I was from life's troubles and difficulties. And yet when I look at some of my colleagues I feel I must have been missing something as I grew up, for they seem familiar with it all and are able to take the bad and the difficult in their strides without a moment's hesitation or thought. Not only have I come to realise that I happen to be different but I am being told and all the time portrayed as different to everyone else. I hate this notion of being singled out. I, myself, see no obvious difference from my colleagues in the way I think or behave. I have spoken to my parents, and in their view people are all different and that I should not much worry about it. "

I offered Giuseppe accommodation for the night, and it was an opportunity for more frank talk. I was appreciative that he had taken the trouble to travel from where he was stationed way south just to see me. I told him about my work and my general life in Sorrento, and about my new love life that was opening for me, a beautiful and attractive girl who was working at the main reception in the Plaza Hotel. I wanted to know more about him and about his circumstances in his new role as an Army Officer. I understood he was facing some difficulties, but he was reluctant to talk about it and I did not press him. He told me he did not think it was something he could not handle.

I said to him " My wise mother used to say - you could never stop troubles coming your way, you ignored the irrelevant ones and they would melt away, but those where the outcome could change the direction your life took for the worse you had to stand up to them and make yourself heard. The way we go about our life and our interests is a fine balance. We try to avoid pain and seek comfort, but we come to realise that however much control over events we think we have, the tables can be turned just suddenly and we are either riding high or thrown into a bottomless pit from which escape can be futile, and it is then that we need to change course before it is too late and when the writing is on the wall. "

I could see how much visiting me meant to him. It was as if he was drawing courage and wisdom for the days ahead. We spent the next morning walking along the high promenade after breakfasting in one of the cafes, and he insisted on visiting the Church of St Anthony of Padua where we both said a little prayer. At midday it was time for him to leave and we said our farewell at the railway station. I returned home brooding over everything and hoped he would succeed and be safe in his new life and the career he had chosen.

The weeks rolled by, I was happy in Sorrento and my job in the accountancy firm suited me well. I was going out with Laura, the desk girl at the Plaza, and life was just perfect. That is until I received a telegram from Mrs Pellaggio asking me to get in touch as a matter of urgency. I dismissed totally from my thoughts that there could be some kind of catastrophe affecting either of my parents as one or the other would have contacted me themselves. I felt apprehensive lest Giuseppe was in some kind of trouble but then I thought that if he were he would have contacted me directly. I put it all down to the logical conclusion of a worried mother whose son had not been in touch for some time and that she hoped I would have some news of him. After all army units are notorious for suddenly moving barracks, and mail tends to be slow reaching home.

I rang the number that I kept in my diary, and not surprisingly it was Mrs Pellaggio at the other end who was obviously waiting anxiously for my call. Her voice was trembling and the words came out interspersed with tearfulness. I asked her if she was alright and if Mr Pellaggio was also alright. When the answer came that they were I felt sudden trepidation that perhaps it was about my parents after all, but she reassured me that it was not. So I inquired about Giuseppe.

She broke down and said " Pietro, I am very worried, I have been crying all day since I received the news. Giuseppe is in prison. Oh my God, why ? Giuseppe cannot harm anyone. It was him on the phone and he could not speak, I think he was not allowed to say much. He said - Mama I am being sent to prison but don't worry, I am innocent. They have charged me with a misdemeanour and there will be a court case. I am being sent today to Anzio, to the Army barracks there where I shall be kept until they hear the case. Well Mama it is not far from Napoli which will help me a lot to think I am near you all. Please don't be upset Mama, it is nothing really. I do not even know what I have done. I have to go now Mama. Tell Papa, and tell also Pietro. Bye Mama. "

" What? Impossible! " I uttered.

Mrs Pellagio was now sobbing at the other end.

" Oh Mrs Pellaggio, do not upset yourself, I am sure it is nothing serious. You and I and everyone who have known Giuseppe know that he can never commit a misdemeanour. I shall ask for time off work tomorrow and travel to Anzio to see Giuseppe, and bring you his news and what it is all about. I am sure there is some misunderstanding. Everything will be fine Mrs Pellaggio, believe me. I shall ask my Mama to visit you. And let us all pray for Giuseppe that Our Lady protects him and he comes through all difficulties unscathed. "

" We shall do anything to get him out of this. Livio will speak to one of his friends who is a lawyer " came her reply.

I promised I would be with her son by midday the next day to find out everything, and would stop at their home on my way back from Anzio.

Mrs Pellaggio's distress upset me. I always looked upon her as my second mother. Giuseppe's news came as a thunderbolt, and I began to feel alarmed for him. I remembered how he looked worried and preoccupied when he visited me, and my fears began to convince me that the difficulties he had mentioned, he was not able to handle as he had hoped and that they progressed beyond a peaceful outcome, and that perhaps he landed himself into some trouble inadvertently and without intent. He is a gentleman in the true sense and does not know the ways of the devious world, and must have got ensnared, which to me was the only explanation.

I prepared myself for the trip in the morrow. I could not sleep that night, and my mind was racing in all directions, trying to figure out what could have happened. Most importantly I was upset for him, for what he was going through or having to endure, and I hoped it would be but a non entity type of a problem and that he would soon be released, and the misunderstanding cleared up.

I reached Anzio a little after midday the next day and made my way directly to the barracks according to the address given to me by Mrs Pellaggio, hailing a taxi from the train station. At the gate they had already advance notice that Giuseppe was receiving a visitor that day, presumably arranged by Mrs Pellaggio who emotionally could not at this time dash to see her son. The formalities to allow me into the barracks were completed smoothly and I was escorted to a one-story building, about twenty metres long in its facade. The escorting soldier and I walked for about four or five minutes before we reached the place. I saw nothing remarkable about the barracks and its array of buildings, very plain and uninspiring. I was led into a waiting room and asked to remain there. It was furnished by two armchairs, and a rectangular table with six chairs. I glanced through the open window at the courtyard and the route we had just walked. I did not know what to expect or what would be Giuseppe's emotional state. My legs felt weak beneath me and my heart was racing. I knew I had to muster my anxiety for his sake. Giuseppe was my one and ever closest friend, and what pained him pained me. Our mutual loyalty has never been in any doubt.

Suddenly the door was opened and in came Giuseppe. Our emotions were so high that we both struggled to contain our tears. We embraced and he motioned me to sit down. He looked at me not saying a word for what seemed like an eternity and finally said

" I knew you would come, and I feel sad no more because I know that I have in you a most wonderful friend, and whatever happens to me, I shall always draw courage from your support and from your solidarity as I have always done. You are the wise one, and I know I can count on you even if it is not within your reach to offer the help I need. Your presence and your belief in me are all what I need and are my constant solace. "

" Hey Pepe, you sound pessimistic, there is nothing that cannot be solved. We will all help you. Your dad is getting a lawyer and I believe they are both coming to see you tomorrow. Your Mama is saying her prayers and will also come to see you. Let's just start by telling me what it is all about. "

' I don't know " came the reply.

" What do you mean you do not know? What is it you are supposed to have committed? "

" I don't know " he said again, " I have not been told ".

" Giuseppe, this is preposterous. You would not be here if they think you have not done anything wrong. I am not saying you did, but surely you should have asked or they may have told you, or is it something daft that you have done and which in the eyes of the Army is an offence ? "

" Pietro, I really do not know anything or why they have arrested me. As you can see I am not exactly in a cell. When my captain summoned me he said that I have committed a misdemeanour and that until this is sorted out through a court martial I am to remain under house arrest. "

He had lost me completely but I believed him. My mind went back to when he visited me in Sorrento and what he had said at the time about some difficulties he was going through. I remembered the worried look on his face and how apprehensive and preoccupied he sounded. I reminded him of this and asked him if there were any events leading up to all this.

Giuseppe opened up as he always did whenever he was upset about something and we were alone, counting on what he called his wise friend to guide and direct him. I knew he had been holding in more than he could bear without sharing, but as he began to recount the events of the previous months I found my emotions surging between anger and sadness, and I wondered how he managed to cope with it all, on his own, in his gentleness and humility, and as he spoke I could glimpse the hurt on his face and in his moist eyes, the hurt that was coming up straight from the heart.

" You know Pietro, I was happy joining the Army. I liked my uniform, and I liked most of all my cap with the plume on top. The training was tough, but I did not mind. We had a captain in charge, the same captain who remained in command of our unit after we graduated. I sensed from the beginning that he had taken a dislike to me. I dismissed it initially and put it down to my imagination, the lack of social experience and some sensitivity on my part. I thought I was doing well in the training and that I was keeping up with everyone if not ahead of some. But he was never pleased. He kept rebuking me, highlighted failings that, and please believe me, were never there and did not exist, and I was always marked down. He let me pass the training however, I am not sure why, and I wish he hadn't. "

He paused and his eyes welled up with some tears. Then he resumed " He beat me a few times ".

I could not contain myself " He what? " I held his arm and exclaimed " You mean he actually hit you ! How could he, the swine ! And why did you not report it, or at least tell us or inform your parents?

" Tell whom Pietro ? And what could my parents have done? " His lips were trembling and I could see his distress as he spoke. " He punched me a few times in my back, during the physical training. I would not have minded it so much if it had not been in front of the others. "

" So he framed you for something he has not told you what it is just to pour more punishment on your head, and likely to get you dismissed afterwards. I think that's despicable and cowardly, and nothing will come out of it, you will fight it and expose the brute. "

" There is more that I have not told you and which I think is at the root of the problem, in collusion with others. I may guess what he has in store for me and what I am probably accused of. "

Giuseppe paused and was thinking deeply. I looked at the beautiful face of this lad I have grown up with, and I felt like whizzing him out of this stupid place. He was tossing everything in his mind, still with that bewildered look, and then suddenly sighed deeply as if he was ready to get it off his chest.

He said to me " What I am about to tell you may seem strange to you, and my conduct in such matters has always been governed by my correct upbringing, and maybe, just maybe, it could have turned out differently had I accepted what I had been asked to do. "

" I am listening " I said.

" The captain is known for his heavy drinking. He does not drink when on duty, but once he is off duty he drinks himself to stupor. He lives outside the barracks among the local community. He managed to get that privilege, for he is married with two young children. I am told his wife is most unhappy about his heavy drinking but puts up with it. But everyone also knows, except his wife, of his liaison with a local girl who works by day inside the barracks as a clerk. One day last month, early evening, an officer knocked on my door - we are housed in kind of studio flats each with en-suite bathroom - and when he came into my room said he needed to discuss a very discreet matter and enlist my help. He went round in circles at first then blurted out the fact that the Captain was at that precise moment completely drunk, that Mima, and that's her name, was with him, and that they did not think he was fit to return to his home at this time, and that they wanted to let him rest in my flat for a couple of hours until he was fit to be taken home, and that Mima will be staying with him until he sobered up. He said I could go to the recreation centre for those couple of hours until it was all sorted out. When I asked him why he chose me, his reply was that he could not find any of the other residents and that I was specifically recommended because of my discretion. Imagine what went through my head, the possibility that the Captain may not sober up till tomorrow, that he is too drunk and starts smashing my place, that I am in collusion about something inappropriate inside the barracks and also behind his wife's back, or that others may become aware of what is happening in my room. My strict upbringing and my inexperience in those awkward matters of life directed me to refuse. My colleague asked me to think carefully, but I re-affirmed my decision. I remember telling him not to involve me in such matters ever again. When I next saw the captain I knew from his face that he had been told of what had happened, presumably by Mima. I learnt later that he was bundled into a taxi home, and that his wife had taken the children and gone to stay with her family a couple of days later, not surprisingly. For the past three weeks my life has been hell, he burdened me with additional duties, I believe he wrote a very unfavourable appraisal about me, and I had a foreboding that I was heading towards an unpleasant situation or that something catastrophic was going to happen to me. "

" So he decided to dream up some charge against you and he sent you here? " I said.

" Not exactly, but along those lines " said Giuseppe.

" He assigned me to the medical centre to be in charge of the clinic, the six-bed bay, and the staff. I was not given any introduction to the way the centre functions or is run, and so I was content to just sit there during my guard shift and watch the happenings. The senior nurse, one of two nurses, carried all master keys to the medication and equipment cupboards. She kept a log book of the narcotic drugs held in the cupboard. On my third day, the lieutenant second in charge of the unit and under the captain, suddenly arrived at the centre, and asked for an inventory of the narcotic drugs. The senior nurse could not find her keys which she said she had left on the desk, and thought they had been lifted, but after some search she found them in one of the drawers of another desk declaring that it was strange. The Officer inspected the drug cupboard with the senior nurse. He concluded that there was a disparity between the quantity present and what he thought there should be. He called for the log book but this was nowhere to be found, after they looked everywhere for it. The senior nurse said she had seen me fiddling with the book that morning. I told them categorically that this was untrue and that I was yet to know what the log book looked like. "

Giuseppe paused, and again he had that bewildered and confused look on his face, that cut into my heart. In a flash I saw it all, but it was only then that Giuseppe began to comprehend the magnitude of those events and their details, and he knew that I understood, and that I was incensed and ready to do battle with him.

" The Lieutenant reported back to the Captain who concluded that an ampoule of a narcotic drug was missing and that he thought it had been taken away. I was dismissed from duty in the centre and asked to report to the Captain in the afternoon. When I did, there was a visiting Major with him, and it was then that he told me I had committed a misdemeanour and that I was to be taken to Anzio and face an investigation. "

After a short pause Giuseppe exclaimed in some distress" Well, it is dawning on me now. Pietro, what am I going to do ? "

I was picturing the dimension of the task before us. In theory things like this do not happen and should never happen. Beside the view that Giuseppe was clearly set up, even by standard norms, everything is usually allowed to resolve once the aim of instilling fear in the intended victim is achieved. Framing someone like that is too obvious and I did not think that in Giuseppe's case it would have stood. Yet, it had to be taken seriously, for Giuseppe was bundled out quickly and away from the manufactured scene of the allegation, and therefore he had lost the initiative to put everything right tactfully and without causing too much of a stir to the captain and his close gang. I put all this before Giuseppe and he agreed with me.

" The whole case rests on the damn log book " I said, " it would have the correct entries for the quantities of narcotics, and we know that any activity would be logged in by date, time, user, and of course signed by two people. We can safely say that neither the doctor nor the junior nurse are in the Captain's pay so to speak, and therefore it is highly improbable the captain would be able to get false entries made in the book. I do not think either that they would have destroyed the log book, but rather kept it in a safe place to be found later accidentally, a convenient way of ending the crisis. Don't you think? "

Giuseppe again nodded in agreement with me.

" But the drugs log book must be produced if we were to end this affair quickly, and once and for all. I hate to think this is hanging over me for some time to come ", was his reply.

At this juncture he became more disheartened and added " Think about the damage to my standing in the unit and about my general reputation. " Then after a moment reflection he said, " How am I going to face Mama and Papa ? "

" Giuseppe, your Mama and Papa love you very much, and they have not doubted you for a single moment. "

It was time to act. I knew he was allowed all comfort where he was held, all meals provided and exercises allowed. I promised to come again, to do everything in my power to help his case, and I reassured him that his parents will be in soon to see him. I tapped him on the shoulder, we embraced, and I wished him well as the soldier came to escort me back to the gate.

In another three hours I was home in Napoli. Travelling from Anzio I kept thinking about Giuseppe and what he had told me, and all the while trying to measure the mammoth task ahead and how to bring an end to this nightmare. My parents were excited and so pleased to see me. I told them I was staying for a couple of days. We talked about my life in Sorrento, but above all we talked about Giuseppe. After supper I went downstairs to see Signor and Signora Pellaggio. Our meeting was quite emotional. They were relieved to hear that their son was being treated well and that he was in a comfortable accommodation with all facilities. Above all they were highly relieved to hear that he was in good spirit and coping well, and looking forward to their visit to Anzio barracks. I related to them everything concerning the allegation and the strained relation between Giuseppe and the Captain, the fault entirely lying with the Captain who has been playing a dirty game on their son. Mr Pellaggio seemed encouraged with the news I was bringing and said he would be feeding his lawyer friend with these details. When Mrs Pellaggio went in to make us some drinks, I told her husband about the physical mistreatment Giuseppe received which he was shocked to hear. We both agreed that this should be kept from Mrs Pellaggio, at least for the time being. When I left them to go up to my parents I could see they were less distressed and less anxious than they were only an hour before.

I could not sleep for some hours and I only nodded off eventually from sheer mental exhaustion. It seemed to me that the Captain's intention was to keep Giuseppe in a limbo for days if not weeks, accused but never charged, on trial but the case never concluded, the finger pointed at but never given a chance to clear his name. And I thought to myself that I have come across this before, that I must have read it somewhere or happened to hear about it, the oldest trick in the world, spreading fear in the heart and mind to control or to punish, and as I lay racking my brain it suddenly clicked, Kafka's hero, the individual on trial perpetually for a crime they did not commit, in fact on a trial for simply being different, on trial for not fitting in, not because of some fault in them or of some misconception, but simply because the others have made up their mind that the individual did not match their conception of life or did fall in with their chosen rigid structure, and therefore they had to be condemned, continually judged and tried, in a never ending game, and however much the individual tried there was no way out of it. And I thought how unjust the world can be, and how cruelly human beings can behave.

I did not wake up until midday. How wonderful it was to be home, among loved ones, and at the receiving end of their unconditional love. But I thought of Giuseppe, of his mental anguish and his loss of freedom, not just the physical freedom but the freedom to trust and have faith in fellow humans, the freedom to think and act independently and without fear of retribution, and mostly the freedom to be accepted the way we are and the way we want to be without prejudice or judgement.

I had to be back in Sorrento the following day, but I was in touch daily with Napoli, and knew of the developments as they happened. It took almost two weeks to get this unfortunate episode resolved, and all the while I was convinced that the Captain was deliberately employing delaying tactics just to inflict the maximum hurt to Giuseppe. The lawyer was on the ball and handled the case shrewdly and impeccably. Needless to say, as I knew intuitively it would come to be, the drugs log book made its appearance, the case against Giuseppe was dismissed, and it was decided that he should be transferred to the Army regional headquarters in Napoli with a promotion to Full Lieutenant. Giuseppe received a letter of apology, and was summoned to meet the Chief of Staff for a verbal apology in person and for reconciliation. They accepted Giuseppe's request to leave the Services, and within six weeks he was out, enjoying life once again as a civilian. He was also in receipt of a modest pension.

But Providence was not satisfied, and fate had something else in store.

After his discharge from the Army Giuseppe spent three months relaxing at home feeling cherished and loved. He had many a long conversation with his mother almost everyday. He tried to map out a future for himself and we discussed this many times over the phone and every time I was back in Napoli to stay with my parents. We resurrected our old days when we were still children, walking up and down Via Toledo, and promenading along the sea front. Finally he made up his mind to follow in his father's footsteps and work for the local council. He was interviewed and appointed as a clerk in the land registry office. He was thrilled with the new job which would bring him everyday face-to-face with Napoli's architecture, inspecting lands, edifices, houses and indeed all types of buildings. I was very pleased for him. I was still living and working in Sorrento. He came to spend a few days with me, and we went out sightseeing, even as far south as Amalfi. They were happy days. We swam in the sea, we dined out, we met with Laura who brought along a companion, and Letizia and Giuseppe got on so well. He was due to start his new job in a week's time.

Giuseppe was always mad about the sea. He liked to swim whenever he got half a chance. During the week prior to commencing his new job he went daily to swim off Napoli's coastline. He was a good swimmer and therefore could ignore the authorities advice to avoid these rocky shores. But I could see his point of view, a quick dip in the salt water, just a few minutes walk from his home. Mrs Pellaggio was always pointing out the dangers unsuccessfully, and wished he would go to one of the proper beaches south of Napoli.

On the Sunday, a day before starting his new career, he decided again to go for a quick dip as he called it. The family were just back from attending mass at the local church across the road. An hour later a policeman turned up at the family's apartment delivering the sad news that Giuseppe had been killed in a diving accident. He hit his head against one of the rocks on the bottom in a shallow area of the sea. When I heard - it was a phone call from my parents - I rushed back immediately. His parents were devastated. The pain we all felt, his parents, myself, was beyond endurance. We followed his coffin into the same church we both attended as children, and we said farewell for the last time at the cemetery. To this day, Mrs Pellaggio visits his tomb daily. And whenever I see Signor and Signora Pellaggio I find myself unable to speak, my eyes fill up with tears, and I simply let myself be embraced by the parents of my one eternal friend.

Life goes on, memories remain, the pain never goes away. To me, Giuseppe was unique in his gentleness, his humility, his innocent desire to be of help, and his zest for life and for fun. His God in the heavens must have decided he was too good and too pure to be left on earth for any time longer to live and struggle in our wicked world. Giuseppe my friend, you are where you belong, immortal, free from all earthly burdens, where there is no more pain, no more sorrow and no more sighing.

****

THE FRENCH WOMAN

My name is Marc. I am 35 years old. Perhaps that is all you need to know about me. Oh, and I am a solicitor by profession. There is nothing spectacular about who I am, just the average sort of man. That is the reason why I am not going to say much about the years that have gone past. My problem is that I have been living alone for a long time, seven years to be precise. The relationships I have had did not last, none of them, and I began to blame myself, that somehow despite all these encounters if nothing has materialised for constancy then it must be me. Sometimes it was them, sometimes it was me, sometimes it was the whole circumstances, and to tell you the truth, not that I did have any problem with the one or two night stand situations, there were plenty of them, it is that I began to despair, it was so artificial, so coarse, it lacked the refinement and the romance, and I wanted feelings, genuine feelings and truthful discourse, not some kind of sensual flirtatious let's get on with it brief relationships.

I heard them in the office where I work - I am not a partner in the firm - I heard them often talk of dating sites, and how people they know have been successful, have had pleasant experiences, even going as far as finding the right person and settling with their chosen partner. It played on my mind for some time, but finally I thought to myself why not, what have I to lose, I could always try, I do not have to divulge everything about myself to begin with, and if it works then for the better. I had tired of the local girls I have been coming across, I felt whenever I was out in the evenings to the social club, that they knew me inside out, every bit of my body, every thought or whim, every like and dislike, and I found it impossible to engage any longer. What was I supposed to do, travel miles from where I live to start all over again, the same pattern, the same delusion, the same animalistic attachment.

So one evening I made myself a drink of scotch on ice and sat downstairs in my little study at home, with my laptop on my knees, searching for dating sites. There were many, some open to all comers, and others specialising for types of people or particular physical needs. Needless to say I opted for the general type of sites, and it was a matter of choosing one. As some were asking far too much information I eliminated them from my search. All I wanted at this stage was a general enquiry with as little personal information to give out as possible. You can therefore imagine how I spent almost an hour searching and eliminating, until I finally decided on Dating Made Simple website. It looked straightforward enough with minimal hassle and prying. All they wanted was a full first and last name, an age, a description of my physical preferences in the woman I want to meet, and a recent photo. The site works by disseminating this information through and it is up to their clients to respond. I had the same opportunity of screening what the site had to offer and I could make the first move if I wanted to. I chose a nice photo taken the year before in Spain, in Marbella to be precise, showing me in off white chinos and pink short sleeved shirt, looking radiant and smiling. I filled the electronic application, switched off my laptop, forgot all about it, and settled in my lounge to watch an old classic The Bride Wore Black, a little gem of a thriller, where the black widow so to speak sets out to take her revenge on the four men responsible for the death of her husband. I enjoyed the movie, slept well and woke up at eight the next morning feeling refreshed and energetic. It was a Saturday.

My notifications for Dating Made Simple was on, so at half past ten I heard the bleep. I checked my laptop and sure enough there was a message. With this dating website you have to log on, using a username and a password which I had set up, to access messages or make contact. It was up to the individual, once hooked, to arrange with the opposite number other means of communication if they so wished. I sat myself down, a cup of coffee on a small side table beside me, and logged on. When I clicked on message, I had one of those life surprises which in my entire life so far I could only count their number on the fingers of one hand.

This is the message I received
' Hello Marc, may be we could talk to each other some time ! '
Above the message was a photo, only the face. I stared at it, it was such a beautiful face, blonde hair, light blue eyes, and a big smile. I kept staring at that gorgeous face, the face of the girl who likely out of many male hopefuls had chosen me.

I am handsome by general male standard, or so I have been led to believe by the various girls I have known and courted. And though I have had my share of very beautiful girls, this face was quite different; it was beautiful beyond measures, the harmonious symmetrical radiant beauty. My mind was troubled, it was now a reality, and it was up to me to proceed or withdraw. I was frozen, I did not have the courage to respond, to leave a little message of acknowledgement, and I eventually logged off. I thought of it the whole Saturday, got on with my usual day activities, going shopping, doing my laundry, tidying up, cooking an evening meal, and catching up on the sports on television. Then I seemed to totally forget about the message, went out in the evening after supper and met some friends, enjoyed the socialising and the wine, and when I returned home it was almost midnight and time to sleep.

When the next day I remembered the message of the day before, it was already early evening. I fetched my laptop, checked my emails, totally relaxing in the armchair in my sitting room, and logged on to the website. There were no new messages, I read the one message that had been sent, looked at the beautiful face, and wondered what to do next. All of a sudden a message emerged, making its way forward, then stopping to gaze at me, which brought me out of my reverie.

' Marc, are you there ? '

After a moment hesitation I typed ' Yes, I am here '
' I am glad I found you. You look a nice person, Marc. '
' Thank you '
' Really, I liked your photo, I am sure that is how you are. '
I mustered my courage and said
' You also come across as a nice person. ' I stopped short of saying how beautiful she was.
I must have paused before sending my message because her next reply was
' Are you there Marc ? '
' I am here. I do not know your name. '
' My name is Eline '
' Oh, that's a beautiful name. It sounds French. '
' I am French '
' You speak very good English for that. '
' I am bilingual. My mother is French but my father is English. '
' I see. '
' I grew up in England, in Tunbridge Wells, but we left for France when I was nine.
' That's in Kent '
' That's right. I do remember many things, I have such wonderful memories of my childhood, playing in the ruins of the Abbey, going to the meadows with my parents for an outdoor picnic, and visiting the church of Charles the First. '
' It is not called Royal Tunbridge Wells for nothing, Eline. '
' Yes '
' Why did your family move ? '
' My mother always wanted to return to her native country, and my father got the opportunity to relocate to Toulon, where I was born, on one of their regular visits to this town to see my grandmother. She died and left my mother the house. So we moved. My father was a tailor, and my mother helped him in his atelier. '
' Is it there where you live now ? '

' Oh no, I moved five years ago after both my parents died, my father first from a heart attack, and a year later my mother from stomach cancer. '
I did not know what to say and remained silent. It was Eline who continued
' My parents were old, they married late. I went to live with my uncle, my mother's brother, but he had a family, and I wanted a way out. '
' Did you not inherit the home ? '
' No, it had so much debt on it. I was left with nothing at all. '

I did not know what to make of all this. I have heard of lots of stories before, and I felt the whole experience daunting, and yet I felt attracted to this woman, to her life story, wanting to know more, wanting to go on talking to her, an inner desire to get to know every minutest detail about her. She had told me so much and I still did not know how old she was.

' Eline, you look in the photo about 22 or 23. '
' I am 25. My parents died when I was 18.
' Where are you now ? '
' I have been in Nice for the past five years. '
' That's a nice place. I have been more than once to this beautiful city. '
' Have you ? May be you can come and see me. '
' Do you miss Toulon ? '
' Not much. If I miss anything it is the sandy beaches and the shingle coves. '
There was a pause and then she added
' I miss my parents. '
' You were orphaned too young, Eline. '
' Indeed. My life has been one long sadness. '

I was thinking what to say next, when suddenly Eline sent me a photo of her. In it, she was reclining in bed, in a flimsy white top and only pink nickers, hugging a dark skinned child in her left arm, a little girl of no more than three or four years who was holding a little book in her hands. In the photo Eline looked extremely beautiful, slightly shorter than the average woman, but with a beautiful shaped body, medium sized bust and attractive legs and feet. I admired most of all her beautiful face with light blue eyes and blonde hair. Then in succession, she sent me two more photos of her, the first a portrait which accentuated her beauty and precise features, and the other a full frontal in a black dress with a gold chain round her neck, and her long blonde hair in tassels over both shoulders. I was mesmerised, I found this girl very attractive, and I thought how lucky I was to stumble on her, or she stumbling on me which was even better as it meant she was keen, and that I was not doing the chasing.

I was still wondering about the child in the first photo, while at the same time staring at Eline's legs.

' Do you like my photos ? ' came the message.
' I do, vey much. '
' It's for your eyes only. I never share photos of myself with anyone. With you it is different, as I feel attracted, I do not know why. I would be very upset if you were to share my photos with anyone else, but I trust you Marc. '
' Do not worry Eline, I am not that type. Actually I am always discreet, and above all loyal. '

She had not told me yet who the child was.

' Sorry Marc, I have to go. Give me 15 minutes and I shall be back. I have to put my daughter to bed. '
' Sure. I shall be waiting. '

I was now feeling somewhat bewildered, almost confused. I revisited everything in my head. The situation so far was that I have been chatting to a half French half English girl, who was born in France and had returned back to her native country after spending her childhood in England, in Tunbridge Wells to be exact. She was orphaned very young, her parents left her destitute, and she had left her uncle's abode to go and settle in Nice. And she also has a daughter, which made me realise that there was even more to learn about Eline, and likely more life complications.

I kept the laptop on, re-unlocking and re-logging, at times losing hope that Eline would make another appearance, but after about half an hour, while still tossing everything over in my head, finally a message appeared

' Hi Marc, I am back. '
' Is your daughter asleep ? '
' Yes, she resisted to begin with, but is finally asleep. I am sorry I took some time. I washed her, and I had to stay with her until she finally fell asleep. '
' You do not have to apologise. Motherhood duties come before anything. '
' If you know how difficult it is to raise a child single handedly, as a single mother, with no help from anyone. '
' I did not know you had a child. '
' I live entirely for her, she is everything that I have in this world, and I would do anything for her, even sacrificing myself. '
' That is very honourable, Eline. She is a lucky little girl. '

I hesitated before adding
' But how come you had her ? ' not adding anything else. I wanted to know more, for the mother and the child do not seem to match.
' You probably notice, Marc, that Nicole and I do not share the same ethnic background. '
' I have noticed. '
' I met her father in Toulon, a year before we moved to Nice. I was working as a chambermaid in a small hotel, and he was in

reception. We fell in love. I adored him. He took me to see his homeland, French Guyana, and we stayed with his mother and two brothers in Cayenne the capital where he is from. I still remember the colourful Creole houses and street markets, and the sandy beaches on the Atlantic ocean. '
' So you married him or lived together ? '
' We did not marry but decided to live together. We moved to Nice, he had some relations there, he got a well paid job, and I stayed at home to look after our daughter, she was born by then. This was four years ago now. '
' Where is he ? '
' He died. '
' How ? '
' In a motorbike accident. '
' Oh, I am so sorry. '
' Every year we travelled back to Guyana, for a holiday, and to see his family. They loved to see Nicole, and his mother was very proud of her grand daughter. '
' And he died in a motorbike accident ? '
' Yes. He was always crazy about riding motorcycles. He wanted to buy one in Nice but we could not afford it yet. We had a small old car. His family always warned him about speeding and stunting but if fell on deaf ears. That fateful day the policeman came to break the news to his mother. I was devastated, totally broken, he was everything I had in life. '
' I am sorry again, Eline. We can change the subject. '

There was a long pause. I could not think of any words or thoughts to convey, and waited. After a while, Eline messaged
' What do you like in me ? '

We were back to romance, I thought. As a general rule, one should not show one's hand too soon, as after all I had no way of checking everything Eline was telling me, but she sounded plausible, and I felt sorry for the girl. I was ten years her senior, quite a gap, but I liked her, I liked what I saw in the photos, and above all I felt on equal terms if not having somewhat the upper hand, and I wanted to tell her the truth, to please her, to give her solace, to lessen her difficulties, and to let her dream. I was dreaming too.

' You are beautiful Eline. I like your looks. You are the kind of girl I am attracted to. You have a beautiful figure. I have already thanked my lucky stars that you have chosen me. I could not have dreamt in a thousand years to meet a girl like you, on the internet it is true, but nevertheless I am lucky enough. '

Was I overdoing it, I asked myself. The words came from my heart, they were not made up, they were not intended just to please, I was truly appreciative and thankful to providence, or my lucky stars, or my fortune, or whatever arranged it that I should get to know this girl. I found her enchanting.

' I am happy you find me beautiful and that you like me. I like you too. '
' Since when have you been alone ? '
' It is over two years now. '

I was still curious. Some things did not add up, and I wanted to know more.

' Pardon me for asking, but have you not had any relationships after you partner's death. There should be a whole queue of men wanting to know you and go out with you. '
' I have decided to devote my life to my daughter. '
' But surely, you are not going to spend the rest of your life on your own. '
' My late partner was everything to me. I felt with him like a queen. He took care of everything in our life. When later I allowed myself to meet up with friends at the local club and to go out in the evening, all I found were men who were only after one thing. '

' But you have gone on a dating site ! '
' I realised I could not go on for ever like that, I need to love and be loved, genuine love, and I decided that a dating website allowed me to do the choosing and not being chased. '
' You chose me, Eline. '
' I did. I felt somehow at ease looking at your face. '
' I feel the same with you. '
' Oh, it is approaching eleven. I must go to bed, I wake up very early to go to work, dropping my daughter at the nursery on my way. Sorry Marc, I have to log off. I shall be online again tomorrow evening. '

I was sorry to see her go, I wanted to go on and on, I liked the girl and our conversation.

' OK. Till tomorrow. Good night. '
" Good night, sweet dreams. '

I was just about to log off when Eline sent me two pairs of red lips which I took for kisses. I sent her back a heart for a reply, my heart, the heart she has touched and given a whole new lease of life to.

I lay in bed, going over everything, what she said, her life story, her circumstances, and the fact that she has a daughter. I knew too much already about Eline, and yet I felt I knew too little. I did not know how and where she lived, what job she was doing, what her financial situation was, and above all we lived in two different countries, it was not like I could drive to see her one weekend. It is true I could fly, but then I would have to stay in some hotel, arrange to meet, may be go to her home if she was willing, and then what, that every time I should need to fly to see her? It was too cumbersome, and on top of this all, there was a daughter, a young child, and a child that certainly would not look to be our child if we were together. My mind was racing, this was something new for me, I had never been in that position before, and I wanted her with all my might, for I liked her. I was apprehensive lest I was being laid astray, it was too good to be true, but I thought to myself that it was so far just an internet acquaintance, and that even if I were to go to Nice and meet up with Eline, I was not committed and I could easily take the flight back, and that was that. Eventually out of sheer tiredness I fell asleep, for I had to be at the office by nine the next morning, fortunately a fifteen minute drive by car.

****

My day at the office was like any other day, the usual house purchase conveyances, land search requests, correspondence with the land registry office, or drawing up wills and testaments. Even though I was quite busy, I could not help but think of the French Woman as I now referred to her in my mind. I felt the urge to talk to her again, to be on my laptop chatting away, gazing at her three photos I had already received, and above all I kept visualising her face, her figure, her legs, and how beautiful she was.

When I got home at the end of my working day, I made myself a quick dish of fresh pasta in olive oil with prawns and squid, tidied up the kitchen, looked into my email, and by seven I sat down with my laptop, logged onto the website waiting for Eline to show up. But it was a long wait that I began to give up altogether any hope of talking to her. I searched the website for her photo but I could not find her. To my understanding, some clients opt to keep their information hidden, so may be I thought the French Woman is doing the same. It was now 8 pm, but I decided to give it another half hour. It was proof, I thought, that I was becoming caught and that the French Woman had ensnared me in her web, but hoping she would not turn out to be a black widow. At half past eight, a message flashed up

' Good evening Marc. '
' Hi Eline, I have been waiting for you. '
' I was also waiting to come online and talk to you, but it takes time to prepare a meal for Nicole, wash her and prepare her for bed. She is playing in her room right now, but I shall have to go in half an hour to tuck her in bed. '
' No problem, as I said to you yesterday, she comes first. '
' How was your day? '
' My day was fine. I am usually back from work by six at the latest, which is seven in the evening your time. '
' What is your job ? '
' I am a lawyer. '
' Ah, you earn a lot of money. '
' Not really. '
' Not like me. Life is tough for me. I struggle to make ends meet from month to month. '
' And what is your job ? '
' I work in a care home for disabled children. '
' That's a dedicated job you have. '
' I like it, because I feel I have a lot to give. I love those children. '
' I can see your devotion from what your are doing for your own daughter. '
' If I could have more children I would. '
' You have been widowed at a very young age for a woman. '
' I still think of him, and of my situation, and I cry when alone. '
' Life goes on. You now have your daughter to love and cherish, and who knows, you might find the right man soon enough. '
' The right man has to love my daughter. '
' Of course. '
' All day today I have been thinking that perhaps finally life is smiling on me. '

Eline took me by surprise. She was going too fast. Even though I was already falling, this kind of thing needs to be approached slowly, with the right romantic build up and the proper temperament, otherwise it burns out before it has even started.

' I am sure things will work out well for you. ' I said.
' With a child round my neck, that is practically impossible. '
' You must give yourself a chance to meet others. '
' If I wanted to be housed and looked after, it would not have been difficult. But I am not like some other women, I don't sell myself.'
' Why did you say that ? '
' It is true. I have been offered, but my mother raised me well. '

She lost me there. I could not understand why she broached a subject like that, and I worried.

' I do not like that kind of talk, unless you are hiding something, and you are not telling me the truth. '
' Don't worry Marc, I was just making the point. I live with my daughter in poverty, unable to make ends meet, but I carry on. '
' It will not always be like this. Things will change, it is the vey nature of life. '
' You can say that because you have no problem. '
' I say it because everyone goes through a rough time or a bad patch, but things have the habit of sorting themselves out. '
' It costs dear to raise a child. She wants to be like all the other girls, be able to go to MacDonald's, have a birthday party, and I buy her toys. '

The chat was going in heavier territories I was not prepared for at this juncture. It was not as if I did not empathise, but I was not yet prepared to face Eline's problems with her. It was too early for me to dwell into these matters or offer guidance or even help. I remained silent.

' Did you think of me to day at work ? ' It was Eline who re-started the conversation.

' I did and I longed for it to be evening so that I could chat to you. ' I said.
' We stop for half an hour between 12.30 and 1 for lunch, and I took myself to a side room, logged on on my mobile hoping to find you but you were not there. '
' I thought of you too, but I did not have the same idea. In any case with the hour difference in time between our two countries I would be working when you stop for your break. I shall keep that in mind. '
' I kept thinking of you and smiling to myself. You are giving me hope in life. Until now, I had decided to withdraw from social life and live only for Nicole. Now I have another person to think of and to want to talk to. '
' Do you like me physically ? You have seen my photo. "
' I love your nose. '
' What, why my nose ? '.
' You have a beautiful roman nose ',
and then after a few moments she added
' All night I longed for some hugs and to feel the warmth of your body next to me. '
' It will be the first thing I shall do when we meet, taking you in my arms and giving you a big squeeze '
' Then come as soon as possible, it has been a long time since I felt the arms of a man around me. '
' I cannot travel right now, I have work commitments. It will be a little while before I can do so. '
' Will you really come to Nice ? '
' Of course I will, but not in the near future. '
' I hope that it is not a few days conversation and then you drop me. '
' Why would I drop you ? Nobody throws away a treasure. '
' Well then look after your treasure. '

I still felt like the whole thing was some kind of mirage. All I had to go by were some photos and some little life stories.

' Eline, why don't we turn our cameras on, and see each other ? '
' Oh, my computer is an old model, and I have no such facility. '
' Where do you live in Nice ? '
' Why do you want to know ? I live in an small apartment with my daughter. '

And suddenly there was another photo that followed her message, of her in indoor clothes combing the child's hair.

' My neighbour took this photo. She is ever so good to us. During the school holidays and the summer she takes care of Nicole. I prepare everything beforehand, her breakfast and lunch, and I drop her in the morning. '
' That's wonderful, you must be very good friends beside being also neighbours. '
' She also picks Nicole up from the nursery school at three and keeps her in her apartment which is right opposite mine until I return from work. '
' A good arrangement. '
' Where in England do you live Marc ? '
' I live in Bournemouth, do you know it ? '
' Is it not in the south ? '
' That's right, on the English Channel. We both live by the sea. '
' Do you live in an apartment ? '
' No I live in a small house all by myself. '
' I can come and look after you. '

I did not respond immediately to the last message, and after a few moments I said
' Does Eline speak English ? '
' No. '
'She looks cute in the photo. '
' She is the light of my eyes. I would do anything for her. '

I had nothing more to say. The French Woman's life circumstances were too complicated for me. But I could not pull out now, I loved her face, I was mesmerised by her beauty, I wanted to see her in the flesh.

' Tell me again Marc, what do you like in me ? '
' I told you yesterday. '
' I want to hear it again. '
' I find you very beautiful Eline. '
I stopped short of adding that I fancied her by my side.
' Excuse me for a few minutes, I must put Eline to bed. '
' Sure. '

I was reflecting, then dreaming, then back to reflecting and assessing, and then again fantasising. I visualised how it could be with Eline living with me, here in England. It would not be a problem for Nicole as she would pick up the English language in no time at all. The French Woman was exquisitely beautiful, extremely attractive, and I also found her charming and warm. As I had decided to keep her, I was now debating with myself the reasons and exploring the best way forward for us together. I knew the decision was taken too fast, but in my soul and in my heart I wanted her.

Eline returned to the screen and said
' She is finally asleep. '
' Do you read to her at bedtime ? '
'Yes indeed. '
' I would like to send you a little book for her if you give me your address. '
' Don't worry about it Marc, and thank you anyhow. '
' No truly, you must know Le Petit Prince by St Exupery. '
' No I don't, what is it about ? '
' That's strange, how come you have not heard of it as a French person. Are you not familiar with French classics ? You must surely have taken them at school in Toulon. '

' I was not good at school, and I left when I was fifteen. I needed the money. I am not educated like you. '
' Never mind, I like you as you are. '
' I know I shall not make you proud, and you need to accept me as I am. But my mother raised me well. I could have gone with whomsoever and earn a living like that but that is not me. '

Again she brought up that taboo subject and it worried me a lot. I could not understand why she was thinking along those lines. I ignored it as I thought to myself the girl is uneducated, and therefore her choice of words is likely to leave a lot to be desired. But that can be taken care of later.

It was time to say good night, and again I received lots of kisses and hearts. I drifted to sleep feeling happy and content, and her photos were the last thing my mind was dwelling on before I lost consciousness.

****

Over the following weeks, I felt the bliss of chatting to Eline every evening, and at weekends it was during the day as well. Our online relationship progressed to an amorous one. Eline informed me one day that she was in love with me in earnest and that she could not believe how she could have fallen head over heels across the net without us meeting at any stage, but that she had heard of many love stories that were born on the net and ended happily. She told me how I had made such difference to her life, had given her hope when she thought life had stripped her of any possibility of it, and that she dreamt day and night of me. I liked to listen to her describing her sentiments and the love she has for me. It tickled my pride, my confidence and my self esteem, and in turn I also felt the joy of offering myself to the French woman, of making it up to her one day for all the suffering she had endured in her life so far, and I started organising in my mind what I should do to bring her and her child over to live with me. Eline sent me three more photos, and I was now completely besotted. She was in a bikini, reclining in a deck chair, with what looks like a cocktail in hand, sipping from a straw. The other photos were of her and Nicole, both in bikinis, doing stretching exercises in one and standing in the pool in the other.

One evening, Eline was very passionate in her messages.
' I love you Marc, I love you with all my heart. I have never loved like this before in my entire life. I am all yours, you can do what you like with me, even if you throw me afterwards, for I shall not complain, I would have lived in heaven, and it would have been my entire life's worth. '
' Eline, have confidence in yourself, why would I throw you, you are my treasure and I plan to keep it, I've told you that before already. '
' I think of you at work, I think of you at night, dreaming that you are beside me, and my body shrieks and yearns for you. '

I wanted to suddenly fly in the air on a magical carpet and be with her. My imagination was spurred on by the photos in her bikini and in her bed clothes I had seen and saved.

' I am going to arrange to fly to Nice in the next month or so. I shall not crowd you in your apartment, but I hope you will join me in the hotel. What will you tell your daughter ? '
' Don't worry about it, I know how to deal with Nicole. '
' Good, all set then. '

It was another day of love conversation like every evening, telling each other how much we were in love, and what we should do when we meet, and the promise of manifesting that love through our physical union. I was riding the silver cloud.

****

When the next evening Eline came online I could sense there was something troubling her.

' Today I was calm and handled the situation well, and thinking of you helped me a lot. '
' What situation ? Are you facing some problems ? '
' I coped as much as I could to try and find a solution. '
' Eline, you are making me anxious. Are you facing problems ? You do not have to tell me if you do not want to. As I was thinking you might join me in England, ideally we do not wish to leave unresolved matters behind in Nice. '
' The landlord came to see me today. He spent some time in my apartment, threatening me with eviction. My neighbour was present which was a great support. '
' Eviction ? '
' Yes, I am six months behind with the rent. '
' Why didn't you tell me before ? '
' I did not want to burden you with my problems. '
' How much do you owe the landlord ? '
' Altogether 3000 euros. '
' That is a lot of money. The rent is 500 euros a month I take it.'
' Yes. '
' What are you going to do ? '
' I don't know. There is a court case against me, it is heard tomorrow, I have received notification, and I must vacate the apartment Friday which is three days away if I cannot settle the debt. '
' But why did you not pay your rent for the past six months ? '
' I struggle to make ends meet, I think I told you, but you did not listen. '
' Can you not start paying again and pay some of the outstanding rent on top every month ? '

' Do you know how much I earn ? All I get on pay day in my hand is 850 euros. Paying 500 euros means I have nothing much left to survive on and to feed my daughter, let alone pay all other bills. I sold the car, I sold some watches I had, I have no one to help me, no family, no support, and I am not prepared to sell myself to survive. My daughter and I will be on the streets come next weekend unless I pay the arrears. '

My French Woman was certainly full of surprises. Was she telling me the truth, was she who she pretended to be, was she conning me, that was all I could think of at that moment. I was thinking hard, my mind was racing, one half of me wanted to help, the other half was telling me I was a fool to think of helping someone whom deep down I did not really know.

' Marc, please help me, send me 3000 euros, you will be helping someone in real need, and saving a child from being thrown onto the streets. '
' Eline, life is not so simple, I hardly know anything about your actual circumstances except what you have told me, and I cannot understand why you have not sought help from the local council. '
' What will the council do ? '
' They surely should help you and house you temporarily. I cannot think of anywhere in Europe where they would allow a mother and a child to go homeless on the streets. '
' Please help me, it will be a loan and I shall repay you the money, I promise, if you really love me, send me a money transfer with Western Union to their branch in Nice and I will collect it. You must do it urgently. I shall give you my surname. It is Chouard, Eline Chouard, that is all you need to enter on the payment, just my name, and give me the reference number, and I can collect the money. '
' What will happen to your furniture and belongings ? '
' They will be confiscated of course towards the amount outstanding. '

' I cannot do this Eline. You are asking something that is extraordinary and at the same time strange. You are telling me you have not been paying your rent, that you will lose your furniture, that the council will not help you, that you will sleep on the streets with your daughter, that you want me to send money via Western Union without knowing any other details about the beneficiary who is supposed to be you, I have no address for you, you have not even given me a phone number, and you want me to acquiesce to your request without any checks or assurances. I am sorry Eline, how do I know you are not a fraudster from the outset, a gang, or some other laundering organisation or drug barons, or that you are appearing in court because of some felony or crime. '

' You think I am some kind of gang or a fraudster, ha, really, you are offending me, and I thought that you loved me, I cannot believe it, if you really loved me you would not hesitate to come to my rescue, I was wrong, I shall have to face my fate, I am not frightened, I have faced dire situations before and I shall face this one. '

I was torn, I wanted to believe her, and I tended to believe her, but my intuition was telling me otherwise, not to be so trusting, she could land me in serious trouble.

' There is no need to be angry. I am sure you understand my situation. All I can do is come and see you, definitely before Friday, see for myself what it is all about, and see if I can be of any help. '

' Just send me the money please, no need for you to come all the way, it is not a big sum for you, I love you Marc, it's only because I love you that I dared ask for your help. '

' You have taken me by surprise. I shall have to think about it overnight and let you know tomorrow. Go to bed now, you must be tired. I must admit that you are scaring me, and I need time to think it over carefully. Good night Eline. '

I logged out not waiting for a reply, I had lost the desire to continue in this conversation. Suddenly everything was upside down, the French Woman was not without heavy troubles and frightening prospects. And it dawned on me that I did not really know her well, that there were too many possibilities and probabilities, that our love story was a scary enterprise, and that I needed a cool head to decide how to proceed next. I fell eventually asleep from mental exhaustion.

I woke up with a headache and a heavy heart. It was Tuesday. Eline was appearing in court. She was losing her rented flat. She did not know where to go. Should I help her and send her the 3000 euros ? at the current exchange rate that is about £2500. Should I trust her ? Should I believe everything she was telling me ? I decided not to do anything. I spent the day at work, but all the while checking in and out on my laptop for any messages. There were none. Once home, I stayed glued for any messages. The whole evening went by and I received none. Was she upset with me, I kept asking myself. Did the judgement go against her, I was wondering. But surely, I kept reassuring myself, the judge would recommend that the council housed her and her daughter. I was sure in my mind that they would see to that. Eline could be declared bankrupt, and the debt would therefore fall and no longer be outstanding, and she could always start again. After all I had some nice plans for her in store. I knew I loved her and that I wanted her by my side, the French Woman in the photos. I went to bed not knowing what had happened. I had no other means of contacting her. I had to wait.

The wait was long coming. Eline did not respond to any of my messages. I begged her to get in touch, I told her I was worried about her welfare and how sorry I was not to come to her rescue. The thought that I had lost her distressed me. I was like a child who had lost his valuable toy. I wanted her by all means, and I was now prepared to do whatever it takes to get her back.

Finally on the Sunday evening my French Woman came online. I told her how much I missed her, how frantically I was worried about their welfare, for her daughter concerned me as much as the mother, and that I loved her deeply and unreservedly.

' You have a funny way of showing your love. You just left me in the lurch, knowing the full consequences. I was mistaken in you, you gave me so much hope, but you let me down miserably. '
' Where are you now ? '
' Why do you want to know ? As if you care. '
' I do care. Tell me what has happened, and I shall try to make it up to you. '
' I lost everything. The little money that I had went on the lawyer I hired, and I do not know where from I shall feed myself or my daughter, there are still a few days till the end of the month. '
' I can send you some money by urgent mail, just to keep going. Give me your address. '
' Honey, why don't you just send me a money order via Western Union, like I told you before. '
' Is your daughter with you ? '
' What do you care about my daughter, you have let her mother down, is that not enough ? You men are all the same. '
' Where are you staying at present ?'
' I am staying with my neighbour's sister on the outskirts of the city, far from my place of work, and even further from my daughter. She stayed behind with my neighbour who is looking after her. There is no place for me, my neighbour is married and the apartment is small. '
' There must be public transport to take you to your place of work. '
' No, I need a car lift, there is no public transport where I am staying, and in any case I have no money. '
' Eline, I plan to come and see you. But I just want to say that everything you are telling me is so negative. It cannot be,

certainly not in France. What you are telling me is too out of the ordinary. Are you somehow hiding something from me ?
' No, I have told you everything. I am destitute, and you did nothing about it when I asked for your help. '
' That is not fair. I did not cause all your problems. They were already there when we met online. What you proposed was not fair to me. I have an unblemished life and a professional standard that I must protect. You came from nowhere and suddenly sprang all this on me. '
' That is true. You can leave me if you want. '
' I do not want to. Listen I shall send you a plane ticket to come to England, it will help you to change scenery. '
' I cannot. The court order means I cannot leave the city. '
' That is very strange. You have been declared bankrupt and evicted. Why the house arrest ? What have you done ? Are you in prison ? Have you committed a crime ?
' Of course not. '
' So why can you not travel ? '
' Don't ask me, ask the judge. '
' Anyhow, you must turn up for work, you need to earn wages. '
' I lost my job. '

At this juncture all my suspicions surfaced once again and I became convinced that my French Woman was in some kind of deep trouble, possibly with the authorities, and all the alarm bells started ringing in my head. But I could not let go, I was by now so deeply attached and madly in love despite everything. I was convincing myself that once whatever was hanging over her head is resolved I could uproot her from where she is and bring over for a new life with me in Bournemouth with her daughter, and I would take care of both of them, and she would take care of me, her man, her rescuer, and she would be mine. I wanted her with all my power, all my heart and all my mind. I could not let go, I was simply besotted and beyond salvage.

' Listen. I am coming. Give me your mobile number and your address. '
' I no longer can afford a mobile. '
' Give me your address then. '
' I can meet you '
' But I need an address in case we miss each other. Come on Eline, you have to be reasonable. '
' I am staying at 36 Avenue Gorbella. The place is not great and the lady I am staying with is not keen on me receiving visitors. '
' I shall meet you in the city centre, but you will have to find a way of getting there. I shall book my ticket and will let you know the date of my arrival and where we should meet. '
' OK. '

She blew me some kisses and I felt that we were reconciled.

****

I managed to find a seat on British Airways flying from Heathrow the following Friday. I was taking a long weekend off, returning on the Monday, which meant two days leave in total. I booked myself at the Negresco Hotel which I was familiar with, as I had been to Nice some years before. I purchased 2000 euros which could be needed I thought, but I was not going to let my French Woman know about it. Hotel stay and other expenses could be covered for on my credit card. I informed Eline when I was travelling and she agreed to meet me on the Saturday down town after her weekly visit to her daughter. We arranged to meet at the Jardin Albert 1er, which is a beautiful park right in the centre where the old city meets the new one, at five in the afternoon. I packed up the best of my clothes, I wanted Eline to see me at my best, first impression being usually the lasting one. The day came and I made my way from Bournemouth by train alighting in Woking, and from there I took the Rail Air Link coach to Heathrow Airport. My flight was at one in the afternoon, so that allowed me to travel in good time, starting a bit early in the morning.

When I landed at Nice- Cote d'Azur International Airport it was two o'clock local time. I took a taxi to the hotel, a ten-minute journey. Halfway along the Promenade des Anglais - the coastal road running beside the Mediterranean shoreline and thus named because in the 1820s it was paid for by local English residents - is Negresco Hotel, a stunning Belle Epoque building with an imposing facade and colourful turrets, and costumed doormen. My room was spacious enough with a side view of the sea. I settled myself in, and as it was still mid afternoon in the month of May when it is light until well after nine in the evening, I decided to go for a walk and to explore the city. I promenaded along the splendid palm tree lined boulevard that stretches three miles, walking along the wide pavement admiring the open sea views, and being met by joggers, cyclists and families, some of them with prams shielding babies and infants. I reached the harbour and decided to climb to the summit of the ruins of the old Chateau, which stands 92 metres above sea level, with stunning views from the top, and an attractive water cascade on which rainbow colours are manifested on the surface of the water in the marvellous sunshine. I spent some time up on the summit and when I made my way down it was early evening. I ventured further into the old town, past the opera house, admiring the old town architecture, until I decided on an inviting looking restaurant where I dined on a sumptuous seafood spread of langoustine, mussels, crabs, sea bass and whitebait, accompanied by salad niceoise over a large glass of one of the best regional red wines, followed by an assortment of the local goat's and sheep's cheeses.

I was trying to relax as much as possible, but the French Woman was on my mind. I did not know what to expect, I was very apprehensive lest there could be further surprises which I was not prepared for. I woke up frequently during he night, worrying and struggling to sleep again. Finally dawn was upon me, and I was up and ready for the day ahead by eight. I went down for breakfast, and although it looked very appetising in its range and its presentation, I had knots in my stomach. I went out for a stroll in the fresh air walking along the Promenade. The sun was already up on the horizon and I could feel its warmth on my face. I had quite some time to kill before the afternoon and so I decided to visit Nice's Russian Cathedral. I remembered from my last time in Nice that it opened its doors at nine in the morning. It was a ten-minute walk from my hotel, and when I reached it I stood, like I did on the last occasion, in awe and amazement at this beautiful fine onion-domed Russian church that is the largest outside Russia. I went in and lost myself in admiration of the multitude of icons studied with precious stones and at the gilded iconostasis, the screen that separates the space for the congregation from that reserved for the clergy. It was by now early afternoon and I stopped on the way back at a nice little restaurant and ordered a Daube de Boeuf, the traditional beef stew of Nice in aromatic brown wine flavoured mushroom sauce and accompanied by freshly made noodles. As I was feeling drained having skipped breakfast, I needed a good meal to recharge myself.

It was by now approaching four in the afternoon, so I decided to go straight to the Jardin Albert and wait for my French Woman to turn up at the appointed time. I ventured right in and sat in a bench opposite its Triton fountain. Behind me was the park's modern outdoor theatre. From where I sat I could glimpse not in the far distance Place Massena, a square of arcaded buildings in stucco style.

I wanted to recollect my thoughts before Eline turned up. I revisited in my head everything that had gone before, and it was all information relayed or gathered through messages. I was yet to meet my French Woman face to face, but I knew what she looked like. I had no clue up to this moment how she talked or behaved, what she sounded like, her voice, her mannerism, her facial features as she talked or laughed, and I was about to find out, and most importantly to take her in my arms, steal a kiss on her lips, and hold hands with her.

As time approached five, checking nervously at my watch, I kept an eye in all directions, looking round me, trying to spot her appearance, but there was no sign of her. There were a few people about, some alone, others in company, but not my woman. As I looked behind me towards the street parallel to the promenade, a pedestrianised shopping area, I thought I saw her. The woman standing about thirty metres away looked like Eline, and she was staring in my direction. As I stood and turned round, our eyes made contact, but she suddenly turned on her heels and headed to her right disappearing in the crowd. I rushed forward to where she had stood, looked in the direction she had taken, but she was no longer there. I decided after all that I must have been mistaken and that this woman was just looking for something else, and happened to stare at me. And yet I had an inner feeling that it was her, and that she could not bring herself to come forward and meet me. I decided to remain in the park, hoping she would return, for what else would she do. But she did not return, and no other woman matching Eline made an appearance either. When I checked my watch again it had turned half past six. I felt despondent, confused, bewildered, and I tried to fathom the whole situation. Eline had agreed to meet me at this hour and in this place, but she had not kept her side of the bargain. Did she not realise I was here to help her, to save her, to offer her a new life and a new hope. I was so close and yet so far, and I had to find a way forward, to find her and to bring a conclusion and a calmness to our relationship.

I got out of my blazer's inside breast pocket the address she had given me, 36 Avenue Gorbella. I went to the taxi stop and gave the driver the address. The journey took about half an hour. I was dropped opposite a five storey building on this wide avenue, which bore number 36. The ground floor was occupied on one side by an estate agent and on the other side by a cafe bar. I did not know which apartment Eline was staying in, so I rang the concierge's button rather than risk any of the other bells. After a little while a French stout woman appeared and unlocking the door inquired about my purpose.

' I am looking for Eline Chouard ' I said.

The concierge's face lit up and she stared at me like in some kind of trance or astonishment.

' Is Monsieur from the clinic ? '
' No I am just a friend. '
' You are not French, and I did not know Mademoiselle Eline had friends. '
' She is expecting me. You can ask her. '
' I am not asking anyone Monsieur. Eline is only here temporarily until they fix a place for her. '
' I know all that Madame. It is urgent that I should see her. '
' D'accord, if you insist. She is on the second floor, all by herself, apartment 6. '
' I thought she was staying with some friend or relative. '
' Oh no Monsieur, the supervisor visited her this morning and has not returned yet for the evening check up. '
' Is Eline alright ? '
' She is stable right now. In fact she went out earlier on and has just come back. You may come in. Remember, you must not

upset her, keep your visit very short, and if you sense the slightest agitation, you must leave her at once or call on me. '
' Is her daughter with her ? '
' Her daughter has been taken into care. '

I did not know what to make of all this. It sounded bizarre, but may be, I thought, that Eline was not feeling well after all the setbacks that she has been enduring.

I climbed the couple of flight of stairs, and knocked at the door marked 6. I was sure I saw an eye peeping through the tiny eye viewer. It was all very silent. I felt my heart sinking, and I was filled with trepidation. Suddenly the door opened, and it was her standing at the threshold, looking at me with her light blue eyes, but her face, the beautiful face, had something weird and diabolic about it, and she had a sardonic smile. I recoiled for an instant, thinking was this the French Woman, the beautiful face, the long blonde hair, the lovely body shape. It was indeed her, the extreme beauty was there but it was adulterated, changed, mismatched, it had an evil look to it.

As I looked at her and as I uttered Eline in a fine whisper, the French woman brought her right hand from behind her back and as she raised her arm I glimpsed in a split second a long knife with a shiny long blade. All I could remember later was my swift reaction as Eline plunged forward to thrust the knife into me, lurching to one side towards the steps leading to the third floor away from the weapon, and grabbing hold of her from the back, twisting the knife out of her hand until it dropped on the floor. I pushed Eline back into her flat and down onto the floor, twisting and paralysing both arms behind her back. By then she was screaming, and her screams sounded like howls. I shouted to the concierge, but people were already coming out of the other three flats on the second floor, and then from the other floors as well. When the concierge appeared, panting from climbing the two flights in a hurry, I explained how Eline tried to kill me.

' She has never done that before. The doctor was here yesterday and they were taking her in soon they said, as they determined she was a risk to herself and that she could not cope on her own, but she has never done that before. '
' Well, I was fortunate. Are you going to call the doctor or the hospital ? '

Eline's howls and groans continued until she was finally removed in an ambulance to be admitted to a psychiatry unit.

The concierge asked me to come in into her tiny abode on the ground floor, and she made me a cup of strong coffee. She must have felt sorry for me, and I thanked my guardian angel that my saga with the French Woman had not ended in me suffering a serious injury or even worse.

' I think I warned you Monsieur before you went up. '
' Not exactly. I did not know she was mentally ill.
' Oh, it has been going on for a while. The nurse supervisor who came to check on her told me she was psychotic. Eline had delusions and she was lately hallucinating. It was very noticeable. First they removed her daughter, but lately they realised she needed more than just medication, or a supervisor visiting everyday. This illness runs in her family you see. '

I thanked the concierge for her hospitality and made my way to Negresco Hotel. I spent the Sunday walking aimlessly, trying to comprehend all that had happened. I was searching for love, and I thought I found it online, but it was not to be. And I was not going to risk it again, you never know what you get next time. But I loved the French Woman, my French Woman, and to this day I have continued to love her. I know it sounds crazy, but I have loved the woman in the photos, the woman that chatted to me, the woman who told me everyday time and time again that she loved me, and who blew me across the Internet kisses and red hearts. I felt good while it lasted, and I feel sad that it has all ended. And yet it could have been different, and it could have had a happy ending, the way I dreamt it and the fantasy I created in my head and in my lonely heart.

****

VLADIMIR

Deirdre Winifred Petrovsky and Daphne Willomena Petrovsky are twin sisters. Their mother Sheilagh Dunne was holidaying in Tuscany with her best friend when she met Vladimir Gregorich Petrovsky. Sheilagh and her friend were staying in Pisa and had decided one day to go to Viareggio and spend the day on the beach. In the space next to their parasol and two deck chairs lay Vladimir in all his majestic inflated muscular body. The year was 1993, four years after the fall of the Berlin Wall and the reunification of Germany. Two years before the Soviet Union had collapsed and Mother Russia stood all on her own. There was Perestroika, and the nouveau riche of the emerging Russia. Vladimir made a kill in the gas business, acquiring fields at bottom rock prices, and became a wealthy man. He moved a large chunk of his cash abroad and decided to settle in Italy. He chose Viareggio and bought a large villa overlooking the sea. To its right stood the large Grand Hotel with its oriental looking facade, and to its left and a little further the Plaza Hotel de Russie. The latter, rather palatial, had been built soon after the Bolshevik Revolution to house the émigré of Russian aristocracy. Vladimir knew all this and dreamt of reviving the old times. Until his villa was renovated and furnished he had stayed at Plaza de Russie. He liked spending most of the days on the beach which he considered top notch. And that is how he met Sheilagh. It was kind of love at first sight. They spotted each other; Sheilagh liked the manly specimen a few metres away from her, Vladimir was ecstatic about the beauty, charm and femininity present all at once in this intelligent and yet vulnerable looking girl. It did not take time for a conversation to be struck, and within a few days and by the time Sheilagh was due to fly back to Dublin, intimacy and love had united them. Vladimir flew to Dublin, they were married a couple of weeks later, and Sheilagh moved to Viareggio to live in the grand villa. A year later, their twins were born and Sheilagh insisted on English names in preference to Masha or Katya. Vladimir was always flying to St Petersburg to look into his business, and Sheilagh accompanied him a couple of times. She admired the

Hermitage, St Isaac Cathedral, Peter and Paul Fortress, and the trips to Peterhof and to Catherine Summer Palace. They were a happy family, and their salon was open to a wide circle of friends and acquaintances who included poets, artists and writers. A few months after Deirdre and Daphne were born, their father travelled to St Petersburg to conclude a business deal never to return again. He was assassinated. It was later disclosed that it was thought the evil deed had come from a business rival. Whether this was true or not, the shock was too great for Sheilagh; it had totally destroyed her new life, and she was engulfed in great sadness. After the period of mourning she decided to move back to Ireland taking with her the twins. The villa was shut but not disposed of. Sheilagh did not marry again, and she devoted her life to her daughters. Both the twins did well, graduating from University, one as a lawyer and the other as a dentist. It was now 2014. Sheilagh was proud of her daughters. But a few months before the time the twins travelled to Viareggio, their mother suddenly collapsed one day and died of a major heart attack. And now the twins were back in Viareggio in search of their father's legacy and heritage.

Deirdre and Daphne upon landing in Galileo Airport in Pisa decided to head straight to Viareggio and stay in the Plaza Hotel, until their villa was ready for living in. They had wired the butler to inform him of the death of their mother and of their sudden decision to settle in Viareggio. The whole machinery at the villa got into full swing, the house keeper, the cook, and a couple of maids, not to mention the gardener and the handyman. The journey by taxi took twenty minutes, and they were installed in a suite with a balcony onto the main road overlooking the sea. Entering the lobby a few minutes earlier they were met by luxury upon luxury, and understood why the hotel was called Plaza De Russie. Only as such it could have been attractive to the Russian Émigré a century before. You were met with an exquisite salon in which hung most beautiful chandeliers. There were paintings and porcelain vases, bronze mantelpiece clocks and Louis XV furniture. Deirdre and Daphne admired the marble flooring. Their suite was just exquisite, with much space and beautiful furniture. It had all means of modern comfort such as remote control of the suite door, and everything else beside, just from a flick of a button on the wall beside the bed. In the evening when dining and in the morning at breakfast they enjoyed the view from the roof top, and the impeccable service.

They were informed the villa would be ready as per their instructions in a week's time. They settled down therefore to a relaxing routine, went for a swim everyday across at Balena beach, sat in Gran Caffe Margherita, and browsed daily the various books at Modenari Libreria. They dined every evening in the hotel's roof terrace in style. And they wondered what sort of a man their father was. They were financially secure, for their mother had inherited all Vladimir's wealth outside Russia. She had also inherited some assets in St Petersburg and elsewhere in that vast country, but had told her daughters that some had been kept from her and had passed on to other parties, but that she did not possess the information on their identity or whereabouts. So the young ladies were continuing in their life of leisure as before. They just wanted to catch up on the past they did not know much about.

Deirdre and Daphne passed a very enjoyable week, lodging at the De Russie. They hired a car, and explored Pisa, Luca and Siena. They did not have time to visit Florence, and had the intention of doing so once they had moved into their villa, which they did at the end of the week.

It was fascination beyond their expectation. The villa was not far from where they were temporarily staying and so they walked the distance. Suddenly they found themselves walking next to a high wall on their right and they realised it must be the perimeter of the villa, until they came to the gate. They turned right to enter through the gate and their eyes beheld one of the most beautiful and fantasy like spectacles. The villa stood towering over a long regal walkway, with marble flooring, and flanked on either side by such an array of dwarf trees and magnificent flower beds. The villa ahead was in four storeys, with winding steps on either side to reach what they envisaged was the first floor, double a person's height above the ground, with below it what they thought was the basement. It had a large semicircle balcony, and all above, retracted further back, were the upper three floors with further balconies and attractive shutters. The rooftop was flat and appeared to hold a terrace that gave a view of the sea expanse.

They were met at the bottom of the steps by their employees, and they went straight in through a door under the large semicircular balcony. This was a ground floor, with a side staircase to the basement, housing the staff and used for laundry and for storage including a wine cellar. They were taken by a lift to inspect every level and every corner of their home. A large beautifully furnished and ornamented salon occupied most of the first floor, with a separate large dining room. They admired the enormous chandelier that hung in the middle, dangling from a high ceiling. The two further upper floors had the bedrooms and separate other rooms used as study or for lounging, and all with a view on the sea. The rooms furniture was modern but with a touch of heritage looks, and there were all means of comfort to the minutest details. Tall bookcases stood in one of the large studies and there were masses of books. Every level had a comprehensive bathroom.

Deirdre and Daphne were overjoyed and they spent their first day roaming round their home to get the measure of it. They felt fascinated by the large library and voiced to each other their intention to go through all the books and find out what caught the interest of their father.

After supper, prepared by their Italian cook, they sat in the balcony of the second floor, and gazed ahead at the sun setting over the sea. It was the perfect sunset and they felt overwhelmed by its beauty. Daphne suddenly said

" There must be documents or the like somewhere in the house, may be in the library, which would perhaps give us a glimpse of the father we have never known. Being here makes me feel so close to him, the father who gave us all this and more".

"You are right Daphne, I love him even though we were deprived of him when we were only infants, and yet, like you, I feel his presence in this house", replied Deirdre. Then she added

"Tomorrow in earnest we start our quest".

Their mother had always told them that she knew very little about their father's past before they met and married. Although she had travelled to Russia with him on a number of occasions, the language barrier and Vladimir's apparent secrecy did not reveal much to her. But she was not concerned for she found in him a kind man, attentive to her emotional needs well before the material ones, and he was definitely generous on both fronts. She was not in need to know much more than the man in front of her as husband and companion. And he did not disappoint her. Deirdre and Daphne knew all this, but after all those years as paternally orphans, they had reached the moment when knowing more about their late father would still supplement somehow the extensive love and support they had received from their late mother. Rummaging one day through the books on one shelf in the library Daphne came across a couple of letters tied together. She removed the ribbon and unfolded them, but she knew straightaway that the words that looked back at her were in the Cyrillic alphabet. She hurried to her sister and showed her her finding. Both remained speechless for a few moments and then exclaimed at the same time that a Russian interpreter would be needed. The caretaker was summoned and was given the task of sorting this one out in the shortest possible time. The man scratched his head and went away trying to figure out where he would find such a scarce commodity in Viareggio and possibly in entire Tuscany.

Deirdre and Daphne had only seen one photo of their father taken with their mother soon after their wedding, which their mother Sheilagh had kept. In it they saw a handsome face with an attractive smile and vibrant eyes. They had always imagined their father as such and had in their childhood and into their adult life built a picture of him that projected pride and admiration.

They kept going back to the library. There were not just books in Russian, but also in German and in French. They found hardly any in English, just a couple, Dickens' Oliver Twist and Stevenson's Dr Jekyll and Mr Hyde, whereas they spotted several of Balzac's among other French novelists and essay writers, and of course great books to the likes of Dostoyevsky, Tolstoy, Turgenev, Pushkin and Chekov, and of Goethe.

"You know", said Daphne, "here is a lifetime of reading, all the classics of France and Russia, all the philosophy that minds have given us, and I would gladly sit and enrich myself just like my father did, for he must have done". Daphne was the intellectual of the two sisters, whereas Deirdre liked to get on with the real world around her but not entirely unmindful of how humanity got there.

While still waiting for a Russian interpreter, they sat down to lunch the next day. They really liked their dining room. There was so much space around the oblong table to move about, it was laid with a cream-colour satin cloth which reflected the light that came through the two large windows, while the silver cutlery shone all the more, and you sat down to a view of the entire sea scape, you did not wish to leave when you had finished your meal

An interpreter was not to be found, for nobody in Viareggio or in the whole district knew or spoke Russian. The locals had not seen any Russians certainly this season. The girls were disappointed with this bit of news that the caretaker brought back, and Daphne began to feel disheartened. Deirdre, the stronger minded of the two, looked at her sister and said

" Listen, we will find everything we need to know even if it meant travelling to St Petersburg."

"I know" was Daphne's emotional reply.

As they were getting up from the table, the butler came in and said

" I am sorry to interrupt you Madam but there is a young fellow at the door who insists on seeing you. He says he is family and his name is Klaus Petrovsky. "

Deirdre and Daphne looked at each other and their faces unmasked the sense of trepidation that had been lurking underneath over the previous few days.

The butler showed the caller in as instructed. Deirdre and Daphne looked on as Klaus stepped into the salon where they had retired after their meal. They saw a young man who could not be more than thirty years old and who had handsome features and blonde hair. He was tall, with deep blue eyes, and a subtle attractive dimple on his chin. He was dressed casually but smartly, and when he spoke his voice was resonant and deep.

For Klaus, the appearance of the twin sisters could not have been further from what he had anticipated. He had imagined them also tall, also with blue eyes and quite fair. What he encountered in front of him were identical twins who had chestnut hair, hazel eyes and who were of medium height.

The sisters motioned to Klaus to sit down. They both sat down opposite him, eyeing him and watching every move. After a few tense moments for both parties, it was Klaus who spoke first.

" I have just flown back from Ireland. I thought I would find you there but they told me at your home that you had decided to move to Viareggio and reopen you home here. "

The sisters looked at each other and the expression on their faces was alike, trying to figure out where all this was leading to, and who exactly their visitor was as a matter of fact.

What Klaus said next came as a bombshell.

" You are my half sisters", he said.

"What" said Deirdre, the pragmatic of the two, "are you saying that you are related to us?" was her reaction. She could not bring herself even to use the word half brother.

Klaus cleared his throat and said

" You did not know about my existence but I knew everything about you ".

The girls were dumfounded. They remained speechless. Klaus continued

" Your mother would have known about it ".

Deirdre felt it was time to get some sense into all this. She hesitated before saying

" So our father was married to your mother before he married our mother " , and after a little pause she added " Our mother never mentioned anything of the like and she would have done had all this you are saying was true. I think you need to come clean and state your motives in all this. "

Deirdre was now decidedly taking control of the situation and this serious matter, and she could not see in it other than someone who is trying to con them.

Klaus remained calm.

" Please allow me to fill you in on my father and our father's life history that you are unaware of. My mother was German, and like many Germans, out of conviction, she had settled in Russia. She met Vladimir when he was still in his twenties, trying to forge some kind of life for himself, and they both fell in love. My father was lucky for he happened to be in the right place at the right time so many times, and quickly made himself. When the old regime fell, he was astute enough to get himself acquainted with the newly emerging post soviet politicians and bureaucrats, and did not shy from offering them his services whenever he could help, at times totally free of charge. He was rewarded with a profitable deal in the gas industry, and with the world changing dramatically in those times, he became a self made billionaire. "

The girls remained attentive, trying to take all this in, not knowing if this was all an invention or some kind of unfolding drama.

Klaus continued

" I was already a small child, and though Vladimir kept visiting us, it was becoming apparent that he was by now distancing himself from us. You see, they were never married. My mother realised that Vladimir was gradually extricating himself from her. His views were by now totally different from my mother's who stuck to her convictions, and general coolness came between them. But he always remained loyal and ensured we had everything we needed. When we heard that he had died, I was then into senior schooling, my mother mourned him for a full year. He left us in his will a fortune, a part of what was his Russian conglomerate. "

Daphne was by now crying, and Deidre put her arm round her. For the girls, it was too much drama unfolding all at once.

Deirdre got up and went to the mantelpiece to pick up the letter in Russian they had found and which she had earlier placed there. She walked back straight to Klaus and gave it to him. Klaus scanned it fast with his eyes and said

" This is a letter my mother must have written when she realised that our Father had relocated to Italy. She is simply saying so and asking him not to forget his son Klaus Vladimirich, my patronymic you see. "

There was silence all round for what seemed like an eternity, and finally it was Klaus who spoke again

" My mother knew of your existence and passed it on to me before she died a few months ago. And so I started my search for you both, I needed to see you and to get to know you. I am not after anything in case you may think so. Whatever you may or may not think or believe, or accept or reject, we are and shall remain half siblings. I went in search of you in Dublin, and from there I traced you to here.

Klaus got up to leave but the girls could see already that his eyes were moist. They, themselves, were now crying. They got up and rushed to him, and all three had an embrace that was full of emotions and belonging. For Deirdre and Daphne it was the conclusion they were looking for, and for Klaus it was finally the recognition he had for so long been waiting for. He did not wish to remain any longer, despite the remonstrations of his sisters, and he promised he would come again.

" I hope one day you will accept my open invitation to visit me in St Petersburg " he said as he was leaving.

It was several days before the twin sisters were able to resume their routine life, for they were overwhelmed to their core. And they felt now an extension from the past to the present and into the future, at its heart their beloved father Vladimir, their mother, and their newly discovered half brother.

AMOS THE PARISIAN

Chapter 1

Amos stood at the bow out on the top deck of the ferry taking him from Calais to Dover, gazing into the distance. He could just make out what looked like blurred terrain, but would have to wait a little longer to see for the first time those white cliffs of Dover he had heard so much about. He had never set foot before in England. His mind wandered and he thought of his childhood in the slums of Paris. Then he saw himself as an adolescent finally coming to terms with everything, his unfortunate upbringing, his inner demons, and the nothingness of his life. He could only understand and reproduce numbers and figures. His friend Berger always told him to get the hell out of Paris and to move across the waters, for it is there he would make his fortune, where his talent with numbers would be appreciated. And now he was on his way, crossing that small stretch of sea, but hoping it would be more than just a small crossing, for he was full of those unsure dreams and giving reality to his hopes. From Dover he would have to make his way to London, that city he has often read about and heard others talk about with such excitement and fever. Berger said it was in the City he would make his fortune, whatever he meant by that.

Some passengers were moving around where he stood, which brought him back to his surroundings. Although the sun was shining, it was a hazy sun for the month of May. He felt caressed by the cool sea breeze, totally different from the stifling heat in the east of Paris, where he handed his rented flat to the concierge that very morning. Until then he had lived on a housing estate, consisting of tall buildings, where people are crammed into small flats, entire families with children and even grandchildren. He was the lucky one for he had a one-bedroom flat all to himself. There was no one else to compete with for the use of the kitchenette and the tiny basic bathroom. He knew he would be swapping past existence for the same as he finds his feet in that dream city. Suddenly his entire short life, at least the part he could remember flashed before him. The gaps would have to be filled with what he was told or made to believe. Amos did not mind all that, for it was about to change, and it had to change, by hook or by crook.

He was an orphan, he knew that well, and he was raised in an orphanage, again he remembered that well. Who were his parents, he will never know. The orphanage keepers never encouraged dwelling on this subject, and it was the same for all the other boys. Although he could hardly remember the day to day life in the orphanage, there were some events which stood out clearly as images in his brain, and there were several of those. He remembered his bed which was tucked in a corner of a large hall right against the wall. He was always scared of falling off the bed during the night, and he hugged the wall as he slept, laying on the outside of him his soft toy the lion which he called Leon. The lion was enough assurance that he would be protected from finding himself one night on the floor, and crying from pain. Did that not happen to Paulo ? He fell and broke his arm, but then he remembered that Paulo was an idiot. He always sat in the same chair in the refectory at meal times. It was not exactly a stand alone chair, for all the chairs were linked together at the bottom. He hated meal times for he was ever apprehensive every time as to what would be on his plate, and he did not like so many things. He always wished he could talk to the cook, but then he never saw that cook. The food was hot enough to be cooked on site, and that cook had strange ideas about food. Madame Legros officiated at meal times, and no boy was allowed to leave the refectory without wiping the plate clean. Amos had a real problem on those days he did not like the cook's dinner. He remembered one day when he was kept behind to finish a plate of petits pois, and was only let up after he cried a lot. But the next day the very plate made its reappearance and Amos had to struggle to eat some of it in order that he gets his ordinary meal for that day. He could not imagine he would miss out on the dessert which was his meal highlight.

Amos stared at the sea, ahead of him the outline of the English coastline was slowly taking form. His mind kept flooding with memories, some sweet, some best be forgotten. He had enjoyed his early years at the orphanage, playing with his mates. He enjoyed the football in the large playground at the back of the main building, but he also enjoyed even more the volleyball that was played daily in the afternoon when the weather allowed. Volleyball was a game for the older boys, yet Amos was able to join in when he was eight, having shown a talent for it, and what pride did he have standing on one side of the net teaming up with the other five players. He was never interested in word games, and reading stories was not for him. Since his early years he had a penchant for numbers. As he grew older, he found he needed to categorise and serialise everything in figures and numbers. He knew that that is when he functions at his best. This became apparent when he started classes at the age of five. Slowly he began to master equations, spatial geometry and permutations. Somehow his brain was made to grasp these formulas when his peers struggled with them. On the other hand, faced with a piece of vocabulary or a dissertation, some simple physics or chemistry, and he would disintegrate totally. And he remembered Monsieur Scarinchi, his teacher in the primary classes. Monsieur Scarinchi would punish him every time he did not perform in the non arithmetic subjects. He often wondered then why the maths teacher would not vouch for him with Monsieur Scarinchi. During the secondary school years, life in the classes was less strict and more supportive. He had his nemesis for some of the lads and some of the tutors. It was then that he self realised he had a penchant for deviousness if given half a chance. He always believed he could forge his path against all odds by deception. Amos did not think deception was against morality. For him, if life does not allow you to move forward, then a little deception does not hurt anyone. Several times between the ages of eight and fifteen he found himself placed with a number of families. He enjoyed some placements and hated others, but always worked his way around it.

Amos was staring at this new land unfolding in front of him. Behind him was his past, ahead of him a new beginning. Was the future certain, he kept asking himself. He would have to take it in his strides, and there was always the charming deception if it came to that. He knew he had what the City needed. He was an IT whiz kid. It was in his brain cells, and in his fingers on the keyboard. Did he really understand it the way it should, or did it come to him so naturally and intuitively ? For him it did not matter one way or the other, he could create and program, design and host, hack and disrupt, and that is all that matters in the IT business. He was now following his friend's advice and advancing as a warrior might do, to gain by merit or pillage by opportunity. And as he became aware of the ferry approaching now fast the English port, he heard the overhead announcements for passengers to return to their cars and disembarkation posts. It was time for his first try in this new chapter, to find a willing driver to give him a lift to London. He was confident, he knew how to spot a likely target, and was able to secure a ride with an elderly man driving a Skoda estate, after all he needed to reduce his expenses as much as he could until he found a job. In no time at all, they got through passport control and customs, and headed for London. The elderly driver was going to drop him in Victoria station. Amos enjoyed the scenery along the route and made some conversation. Two hours later he was standing in Victoria station with his hand luggage on wheels. It was a strange world and yet it was not that different from the city he had just left. It was 7 pm.

Amos had just completed his eighteenth birthday. The orphanage had allowed him to leave and start his life independently. He had managed to obtain his Baccalaureate. He was six foot tall, with an oval face and a large forehead. He had deeply set blue eyes, chestnut frizzy hair, and broad shoulders. He was never one to wear formal clothes and he was more comfortable in casual outfits. He liked classic tailoring and comfortable shoes.

Amos was looking round him, taking everything in, observing and analysing. His brain always worked that way, searching as it analyses, the way a computer works. He needed a place to stay, cheap but safe, clean and central enough. As he pondered, suddenly he heard a man's voice saying

" Are you new in this part of the world ?"

Amos looked round and saw a man of about thirty, well presented in his attire, certainly not from the high street shops, clean shaven, grinning at him. Amos replied

" I was looking for a hotel or a motel, or even bed and breakfast for the night. "

" I am Tony ", said his companion, " I come here most days looking for a lodger. I have a house in Finsbury Park, and I rent a second bedroom which helps with my mortgage. It is not expensive, only fifteen pounds a night, and that includes breakfast. I leave for work at 10.30 for I do a late shift, and that is when you will have to leave as well. "

Amos was relieved his first day had sorted itself out so smoothly and agreed. Forty minutes later he was in his overnight lodging. It was a two bedroom end-terraced house, modestly furnished. Tony offered Amos a cup of tea, and Amos ate a tuna sandwich he had bought on the ferry. Amos gave Tony the minimum details about himself. He was now tired, and retreated to his bedroom. He had just enough energy left to brush his teeth and change into his pyjamas. A few minutes later he was fast asleep. Before nodding off, he was satisfied he had his personal documents and money on his person in bed, and that he did not need to get up till 9 am, thus enjoying a good night sleep to re-charge his energy and stamina levels for the next day. It was approaching 10 pm.

Chapter 2

Amos stood on the pavement facing the large glass windows of a job agency. It was time to start his hunt in earnest. He had been in London 48 hours and had managed to find a studio flat in Earl's Court at a modest rent. Tony had dropped him back in Victoria Station only the previous morning with a copy of the Evening Standard, and he had spent several hours looking up, weighing and answering advertisements for a suitable accommodation. Finally he was settled in what was no much different from the one he had left in Paris. The room was spacious enough to move about, to sit and relax, or to lay his possessions in the open. It had a single bed, a round table, high enough to serve for dining and for writing, with two simple chairs. There was also a small armchair, a hanger stand, a waste basket, and a two-compartment built-in wardrobe. A large hollow in the wall on the opposite side of the bed was to serve as his kitchenette. It had a small flat electric stove, with a little surface to its right housing a kettle and a toaster. A couple of drawers underneath had cutlery, and a small overhead cupboard had adequate crockery. There was a sink to the left, and a tiny fridge you squat to reach. In the far corner, next to the built-in wardrobe, stood the walk-in shower cubicle. Amos thought this was perfect. He had spent the day arranging and settling himself in his digs, went for a walk round the block to acclimatise himself with his neighbourhood, and to discover what it had to offer in terms of life facilities. He had spotted a couple of job agencies, and he was now standing, the next day, opposite one he had ear marked, ready to go in and take the bull by the horns.

Amos had been debating with himself the reason he had swapped Paris for London. He kept going over the real reasons he had decided to leave what he was familiar with for the unknown, and certainly this was unknown quantity. His brain was only able to think logically if he applied such mathematical terms to his thoughts. He knew he had to make a new start, a fresh one to be more precise, and fresh starts are the backbones of success. He knew that, beside diplomas, anything else of the person's background or circumstances, when they are of no attraction to life changers, would be best dropped as history, and you move in a new sphere, acquiring a new history, a semi-quasi new identity. He could have made a career in Paris, after all IT is sought after everywhere, but he was sure the psychological impact of his upbringing would follow him, outwardly and inwardly, his reaction and the world's reaction, whereas in London, he was removed from all that, as if the yoke he was harnessed to had been lifted off his shoulders. He had good intentions, but if the world plays dirty, for according to him the world is unfair, then he would play the same game. In fact, he thought, if the world is fool, then he gets to win, for he had no compassion for foolishness.

Amos went in. The agency was deceptively spacious which appealed to him. He had always liked big space, and had dreamt of occupying an office just like that. There were three large desks, two in parallel to one another on the left and the third desk separate from the other two and on the right. Amos glimpsed in a flitting moment three badges. Fiona and Kevin occupied the desks on the left, and Hayley sat all by herself on the right. He found it a little surprising that there were no clients, but then he realised that private agencies dealt exclusively with investments institutions, something governmental job centres did not. He liked the look of Hayley, a voluptuous blonde with short hair and a big grin, wearing a floral dress, radiating optimism all around her. Amos conducted himself well, presented his credentials in a well structured manner which impressed Hayley. She was an experienced hirer and could tell within a few minutes of chatting with someone whether she was onto a winner. She outlined the couple of clients she had on their books, and promised to make the necessary contact, and would be ringing him with news. Amos had purchased a SIM card as a matter of priority.

He walked out after half an hour, and sampled life around him. He liked what he saw. People were bustling about, some briskly, others leisurely. He wandered around, eyed all the shops and restaurants arranged in two rows, either side of the main street, and studied the traffic of cars, buses and pedestrians. He ventured into a Simply Food store and bought some provisions for the next couple of days. He enjoyed breathing in the fresh air, and made his way on foot to his flat, a few hundred metres away. He spent the next couple of days at home, reading in his French book, Notre Cœur, a short novel by Maupassant.

Two days later, Hayley was on the phone. He had an interview the next day with an IT company in the City, near Liverpool Street. Hayley wished him good luck and stressed the importance of demonstrating his computing skills as the competition was fierce, and she knew of at least one other strong candidate. Amos reflected over what Hayley said on the phone. He felt confident enough, and rummaged through his head ways and manoeuvres to charm his way whilst at the same time displaying his unusual skills. He would see to it all tomorrow, and reminded himself that the purpose was to secure the position, and that as Machiavelli wrote in The Prince, the end justifies the means.

Chapter 3

Amos sat at his desk, one of many in a large hall. The one he occupied was near one of the large windows, and so he could glance out anytime he liked, whenever he looked up from his desktop or managed a side glance as he worked. He did not mind that the view was the side wall of the next building, an investment bank, with also so many windows looking onto the courtyard that separated the two. It was Monday, and Amos had already been working for his new employer for a week. He paused and reflected on how fortunate he had been so far. Providence had propelled him so quickly, as if everything had been pre-ordained. Ten days before he had come for the interview and he was met by Guy and Susanna. The interview went smoothly, he had the impression that the company was desperate for skilled staff, and after preliminarily friendliness and general enquiries, it was time to answer technical questions on IT practicalities, mainly programming, followed by practical demonstration. He knew he had sailed through. He did not like Guy much, he struck him as a smoother and a devious person. Susanna introduced herself as one of the managers, and after he was offered the job, confirmed she would be his direct line manager. All the previous week, Amos had been assigned work on on-going projects, and he duly obliged them with the goods. He was beginning to grasp the concepts behind market needs and how business websites are set up. For him there were big profits to be made, and it was such companies as the one he worked for which made the kill. Amos gazed out of his window at the walls in front of him, and in an instant planned it all. He was just biding his time.

One day, after leaving work, he made for the local pub, the Stag's Head, for a lager. It had been quite warm, and he felt he needed to relax after a particularly heavy day at the office. That day Susanna was irritable and irritating as usual, and most of his colleagues struggled to cope with her. You never knew what she wanted from you, it always looked as if her change in mood and of instructions were a direct result of some issues filtering down from her superiors. He felt that behind the calm smile, there was panic and worse still, there was lack of integrity. But then he thought to himself that this was the way of the world, the way of businesses and institutions, and that the pragmatic way was to absorb such masked aggression until the day that tables are turned. As he drank his beer, he felt held in each elbow by a hand. He looked one way and then the other, and was surprised to see Susanna and another woman which she introduced as Angelica who worked in the executive office of the company.

Susanna and Angelica joined him for a drink. He tried to compare the two who physically were quite different but who appeared to be very close friends and who, through their laughter and their reciprocated banter, gave the impression they were in collusion. It was as if he was noticing Susanna for the very first time. She was fair, tall by female standards, had greyish green eyes, black hair, and her clothes imparted a failing effort at dressing well. By contrast, Angelica was short, round, had chestnut hair and blue eyes, and was loud and unrefined.
It was Angelica who suddenly put a stop to the empty chat and said " So Amos, how do you find work? ".
Amos gave a diplomatic answer.
" You know Amos " , said Angelica, " there are great opportunities in what we do, the company is doing well and is winning new contracts, and I think the likes of you stand to benefit much and to rise to great heights . "
" I am quite happy ", said Amos.
Angelica looked at Susanna, and they both seemed to exchange subtle smiling eyes, before Angelica turned to Amos and said

" A company like ours relies on bullies. We need bullies to keep workers on their tiptoes, and to win market contracts from other competitors. Are you a bully Amos ? "
" I can be. "
" I am sure you can, Amos, and I have all confidence in your abilities ", said Angelica. " By the way, you can call me Angie ".
" Angie is the real force behind our projects " said Susanna, and gave Amos a wink.
Amos kept the two women company for another half hour, talking television soaps and such other non sense, the only topics which seemed to fire them up. When he left, they were still chatting merrily over the remainder of the bottle of wine they had bought. Amos returned home, and all evening kept thinking of what to make of that devil of Angelica. Was she trying to get a feel of his psyche or was she setting a trap for him ? He tried to figure them out. As far as he could see, they were the two witches he will have to deal with, and he realised it was not an easy task. If only, he thought, he could one day rise to the top, perhaps he could harness their wickedness to his benefit. For the time being he knew he would have to keep his head down and play their game.

Chapter 4

The weeks followed each other and Amos settled to his job well. His task was to create websites for businesses, and this meant many lengthy meetings with entrepreneurs and also with some upwardly aspiring amateurs. Towards this, he needed to collaborate often with Julie who occupied a desk right at the opposite corner from where his desk was in the big hall. Julie had been in the company for almost two years, and she was tasked with designing website pages and website screens. It was the like of Amos who then put it all together and made it fully functional, with all its features of home, menu, basket, payment, and whatever else the client needed. Amos enjoyed working with Julie and began to look forward to the time of the day when they would be working together on the going project.

Julie was not only beautiful but the sort of beauty Amos felt attracted to. She was twenty-one years old, two years older than Amos who was fast approaching his nineteenth birthday, but for him that did not matter. Julie was just the right height for any man., her body was shapely and had all the right curves in the right places at the right size. When she looked at you her light brown eyes sparkled and seemed to talk to you. Her face was slender, with a dimple on either side, her hair was black, and her skin was white with a touch of rosiness in her soft cheeks. She had perfectly shaped slender fingers, and she wore cyclamen nail polish. Amos liked Julie's dress sense, her clothes were radiant in their muted colours, and the couture she chose made her look unique when next to other girls. Although Julie maintained the professional cooperation at all times, Amos felt of late that the admiration was mutual. And so de decided one day he would ask her over for dinner. He could cook the perfect ratatouille.

Amos was delayed in finishing his work one day, and it was approaching 6 pm when he left the office. Unknown to him, also Julie had been kept back by a meeting with her boss, and so they met each other as they stepped out of the building into the street. They walked side by side, Julie was friendly as usual and brimming with her infectious smile.
Amos mustered all the courage and the confidence he could find and said
" I don't know how to say this but I would like to invite you over for a meal. Will you come ? "
" Yes, I will come " came the reply, without any hesitation.
Julie looked at Amos with that look that says: I am a modern woman. I can take care of myself.
" I would like to get to know you. I like talking to people and I am sure I will enjoy your cooking. "
They agreed the supper date for Friday evening. Amos gave Julie the directions to his home. He had moved from his tiny flat in Earl's Court to Bromley where he rented a small end terraced house, and had bought a small Hi-Fi, and a few prints to hang on the walls, as well as some decorative vases and small trays.

Friday came, and Amos was all excitement . He managed to get home soon after leaving work at five, and started straightaway on his ratatouille. He had come to perfect a slight variation of the recipe, adding, in addition to the various vegetables, lean chicken breasts cut in small portions. The secret was in the timing of the addition of the various ingredients during the frying stage, until the tomato juice is finally added, and the whole mix spiced with Provence herbs. Then he laid the table as best he could. He had prepared a bootle of red Bordeaux to go with it, and kept next to the CD player on his Hi-Fi, to be played later, Faure's violin sonatas, which he liked much and which he thought would compliment well the ambiance.

Julie arrived at seven, looking exquisitely beautiful. She was relaxed, talkative, enchanting, and radiating confidence and warmth. They sat down to their meal. She complimented him on the ratatouille and the tasty rice he had also cooked. She liked the red wine, and was drinking it heartily.

After a while Julie said " Tell me about yourself. "
" There is nothing much to say, what you see is the real me. I am French but I find it fascinating living in London, and I intend to stay and work here. Perhaps you should tell me about yourself. "
Julie stared at Amos for a few moments then said
" I am a single child, and I have the most wonderful parents. You can imagine what I am for them. They have instilled in me the exploring mind that you see in front of you and the confidence with which to tackle everything in life. In our family love permeates everything and everyone. We are all so attached to one another and yet each one retains their total freedom as individual without undue pressure or enforcement. That is the magic of our family, we are committed, we care, we are close, and love is all around, and at the same time each one of us is able to enjoy life in its vast knowledge and activities. In fact we share in what we like a lot of things. We share above all a strong faith in the Almighty which we believe sustains and nourishes us in ways not possible otherwise. "
Amos listened to Julie and wished he had known in his life what she was now talking to him about. He knew he was different, not only in his circumstances but also in his heart. Compassion, love, solidarity with others, had never touched him the way Julie was explaining to him. For the moment he wanted to enjoy Julie's company, and he really was.
" Tell me, is there anyone in your life, other than your parents? " he said to her.
" No. I knew once a young man over a few days, but he was not the right person for me. I am saving myself, for I am sure I shall meet the right man one day. "

After a moment's hesitation she said playfully
" There is someone right now, but I do not know much about him. I shall have to wait and see. "
And her light brown eyes sparkled even more and played havoc with Amos.
" I like this piece of music. The violin is so beautiful. ", Julie said, referring to Faure's sonata which was playing in the background.
Amos invited her to dance and she obliged. He held her by her right hand with his left hand, and his right hand was round her waist, and he felt mesmerised, a sensation he had not experienced before, though he had been out with some girls back in Paris as a teenage boy. He tried to kiss her gently but she stopped him and said
" I don't want that. "
Amos was not upset, on the contrary he felt very happy. Time flew and it was approaching 11 pm. Julie said she should go as it was already late, she would take the train to central London and then the tube to her flat in South Kensington. Amos walked her to the train station. Once back home and in bed, he reflected on the beautiful evening he had spent with this wonderful girl, and hoped their friendly relationship would continue to develop, and who knows, Julie might even fall in love with him, but he was not sure he was ready for such a course. And as he fell asleep he was still debating with himself whether love and passion were a requirement for mutual understanding and partnership.

Chapter 5

Amos reached his first anniversary with the company. He was deemed indispensable by his colleagues to the smooth closure of all the projects they were working on. They saw him as genuinely clever in IT matters, and would seek his help whenever they came unstuck in what they were doing. Amos never held back, and coming to the rescue of his colleagues satisfied his vanity and his inner sense of achievement and of power control. But for him this was not enough. He craved more success, and his aim was to reach the top of the echelon. There were obstacles, and he knew that these obstacles were not about talent or merit, nor about lack of opportunities or budget constraints, but that they came from rivalry, and rivalry at its worst, the kind of rivalry that generates spite and contempt from others, when they realise there could only be one place and one winner. And he had Susanna on his back, day in day out, making life difficult, alienating him from his colleagues and other staff, marginalising him whenever there was an occasion where he would shine, ensuring he has been excluded from the event.

The problem, as Amos saw it, was that Angelica was the real back seat driver, seizing on Susanna's lack of confidence and general indecision, taking all the floor decisions herself and filling Susanna's head with her twisted vision of how things around should be. It was Angelica who always suggested to Susanna whom she should promote or trust, and you would see her often in Susanna's office dishing her dirty tricks and catching up on the malign gossip. She had a revulsion for anyone who showed independence of mind and intellectual ability. Amos, despite his younger years understood all this, and could see through the pair of them. He knew that each problem he encountered at work was manufactured in Angelica's head, and that her style was to undermine whoever she thought would be a rival to her. She wanted to climb to the top and stay at the top. Susanna was her runner, and for her loyalty she would see that she would be recompensed with a cushy position when such position arose in the company. For the moment Amos would have to endure the silly daily emails and the intermittent aggressive face-to-face encounters, the sole purpose of which was to unsettle him and may be force him to quit.

Amos continued to work with Julie. They went out together a few times, but the relationship stagnated at the friendship level, and this was entirely Julie's decision.

Amos saw Guy a few times. A tall man, always smartly attired in a suit, Guy was on the exterior a pleasant person to get to know, talk to and work with. But the rumour was that he was deep down a nasty person, and that should you one day resign your job and try to move on, never rely on a reference from him. He was notorious for ruining it for the person, and it remained a mystery as to why he should behave in this way. Amos always laughed inside him at this and thought Freud would have a field of a day trying to analyse Guy's behaviour. He tried to remain on good terms with him, and on many an occasion did actually have interesting conversations with Guy, talking about travels, the theatre, financial enterprises, politics, and IT science, which he did enjoy. He found Guy xenophobic who did not like anything un-English, but he did not mind Amos's background culture and heritage, and in fact showed respect and admiration to some of his francophone dimension. Guy was on the board and a major partner in the firm, and so carried a big weight and could make it or break it for you according to his whims. He was sure if it were not for Guy on the job interview he probably would not have got the job. Amos wanted to be like Guy, to own and to control, and he realised that he would have to seek a parallel way or method of some kind to fulfil that ambition, but he could not fathom yet how he would do this.

Amos did not find it easy working in that kind of atmosphere. It weighed on his mind and his heart, and were it not for his work friendship with Mark who occupied the next desk to his but one, he would have found the going in the office intolerable on many days. He enjoyed his work, but he also enjoyed the flair and the freshness of spirit that Mark brought with him. He enjoyed stolen moments during the working day when Mark and he could discuss art and philosophise about general or specific topics. Mark spoke good French and could hold himself in that language quite well, which helped their verbal exchange when they did not wish the information to be shared with the others. Marc was Un Homme de Lettres as Amos would say about him. He was knowledgeable on English, French and Russian literature, he frequently went to the opera or watched ballet on stage, and he was a frequent visitor to museums and art galleries. He had done much travelling abroad and was therefore conversant with the ways and customs of many nations. Mark brought to the office a sense of freshness that was needed to dispel the stifling and the bullying from management that bordered on negativity. Amos and Mark often discussed heroes and heroines of famous novels and stage dramas as well as general metaphysical and philosophical ideas.

Amos admired Mark and would often quiz him about artistic knowledge. Mark seemed always to have a ready reply, and his way of explaining things held your attention and kept you interested. Amos regretted he did not have artistic hobbies like Mark and made a resolution to make a start, for he was still very young and if he began now, in the long run he would have that extra depth that he so much admired in Mark.

Mark was down to earth. He was a handsome man, his features had symmetry and harmony, the quintessential basis for beauty, and his body proportions were ideal, neither stocky nor thin, neither excessively muscular nor skinny, but of handsomeness that caught your eyes. He was very popular with the ladies, and their great regret was that he was married and was a good family man with two adorable young children.

Mark often repeated to Amos: " Knowledge puts you on a different plain from others. Suddenly you realise that what matters most in life is that extra perception, that additional sense, and you are able to step back from it all and see the global picture, understand what it is all about, feel people's turmoil and anguish, grasp and comprehend the meaning of our existence, cherish the suffering that we have to endure on earth, and rise above all materialistic attachments to break free in mind and reason. "

Amos often wondered at those words. He would accuse Mark of not being pragmatic and of being a dreamer. Marc would reply " There is no more reality than what I have described. Reality is within us, is our reason, is in our struggle to understand the essence of life. You and I do not have that extra sensitivity that artists and writers have been endowed with and who in a few words, in a few brush strokes, in a few musical notes, are able to say what you and I would struggle to eternity to describe, and when it is all said and expressed, we suddenly understand, suddenly see it all, and know that what we have been experiencing in our hearts and our minds has just been said, and we feel happy and delighted that it is finally out, and that we can agree about it. Art portrays true reality, the reality that is around us and which we may not experience in its totality but which nevertheless exists. We live in a fast flowing world, where everything has a materialistic value at the expense of our inner self, and where strife abounds, and the anxiety that comes with life's struggle and its boredom pervades all walks. Wasn't it Nietzsche who said - We have art in order not to die of the truth ? - Art has always been with us since early civilisations, and will always continue for it is an integral part of our living on earth, and I see no conflict at all with not being able to live in reality. "

Amos enjoyed those chatting times, and reflected afterwards a lot about what was said. But he knew deep down that he was not endowed with such sensitivity, and that reality for him was not in rising above it all but to be on the ground, a foot soldier fighting his corner, and that if it came to push and shove then he would proceed without any hesitation, taking the only course that the world around him understood well.

Chapter 6

The rumour spread quickly that Guy was looking to sell some or all of his holdings in the company. He must have needed the cash to start some other project or perhaps for a big spend. The weeks that followed saw frantic activity in the boardroom, with many visitors to Guy's office. This became the main topic of discussion among the staff. It was a worrying time lest Guy should sell the whole company, for no-one believed deep down that there were other so called anonymous shareholders, and they were certain that the company belonged to him in its entirety. A new boss meant big changes, which would not be welcome, with all the uncertainties that this would bring. Angelica, in particular, was greatly disturbed that, with a new management, she would be sent back to the desks, where she would seriously struggle at work. Chance does not repeat itself twice, she had forged her way to the executive level through cunning and deception, coasting along other people's hard work, attributing to herself ideas not of her own which she amalgamated as if they were her brain child, and which she incorporated in her presentations and formulations. Amos had been incensed on two occasions when he found out some design ideas he was working on had suddenly appeared in Angelica's submissions to the board about new directions for the work line. Angelica was determined to stay at the top at all costs, and was aspiring to even going higher.

Amos also had ambitions of his own. He wanted to emulate Guy and one day own his own company. So far he had only managed to make modest savings from overtime work and from bonuses, amounting to a few thousand pounds. That is hardly the capital you could do something with. He had bought a small property in the area where he used to rent, and he considered his mortgage serviceable whatever the circumstances. He was astute and wise when it came to financial matters. He had managed to furnish his small house with all the essentials. He knew that business success relied on capital and turnover. He needed the capital first, and he was not prepared to wait years to build it up bit by bit, when inflation would erode into it. He wanted it now, and he thought of the opportunity that arose with Guy offering to sell 25% of his share.

Amos had been for some time playing the lottery but he never managed to win anything. One day as he was passing a betting shop, he was curious to go in and find out what they had to offer, for his flirting with the lottery had been disappointing. He was surprised to see so many men, some watching results on screens, others watching live horse racing, and others browsing through leaflets and newspapers and filling forms. And he thought to himself: do these people come here because that is what makes them tick, or are they like me after some kind of dream in their lives that cannot be reached without substantial financing which betting kept their hope alive? He decided to trust providence, it had been good to him when he first landed in this country, and he was now depending once more on its support. He spent some time studying the various options on the shelves, rummaging through pamphlets and forms, and finally decided he would play the odds of predicting ten football match results in terms of a win, all his selected winning teams achieving it in succession. With quick mental arithmetic he calculated, after looking at the odds for each match, that ten pounds could produce a huge windfall, provided that the results came out for a win to the team he chose in each of the ten matches without fail. He filled his form, took it to the punter, paid his ten pounds, and got a receipt showing the odds and the teams and matches. It was Friday, the matches were being played over the weekend, and he would have to wait and check the results online as they came out.

In the months that preceded, business was slowing down as market demands for IT solutions were drying up. Guy recognised the effects of a blip recession, and was waiting for business to pick up again. He did not like seeing his employees sit idle, gossiping over cups of coffee. This period was no more than a blip, and sure enough IT activities and demands increased, and Guy hoped business would return to its previous level. A company called Textile Technology, which supplied material designs to clothing manufacturers, was expanding rapidly, and they needed a sophisticated IT website that could reach out to all its current customers and attract new customers through efficient, fast flowing and modern web pages. Guy saw this opportunity as crucial to the future of his company and its ability to compete and secure contracts. If he were to win such contract, the company market value would rise and he could make his kill and sell off in due course. He looked around him, and saw only mediocrities in his managerial staff. He was never able to hire 'La crème de la crème' and could never entice such labour to defect from other companies. Knowing what Amos could do when it came to web designing he always felt a twang that this young man could outdo him in that field. But he needed him and he could think of no-one else to trust in the preparation of his response to the tendering by Textile Technology.

Guy sent for Amos and asked him to come to his office. Angelica knew of this development almost immediately through the little spies who had sold their souls long ago, the information reaching her via her aide-de-camp Susanna. Everyone in the company knew of the existence of this hateful pyramid, and judged what they said or did accordingly. Angelica loathed Amos, and she was not going to let him now steel the show if it turned out there was something in it.

Amos knocked on the door and went in when he heard Guy's ' come in '. Guy asked him to sit down, and started his usual preliminaries of pleasantries and general inquiries, which Amos was quite familiar with and which he knew meant there was a serious and important matter at hand.

" Tell me Amos, how would you feel if I kind of promoted you, to work close by my office, on a new project I really would like you to work on and which means a lot to me ? "

Amos waited for the continuation but this did not come. It was typical Guy, he thought, and he was obviously waiting for an answer. The two men stared at each other, weighing each other up. Finally, Amos replied: " Sure, I do whatever job you allocate me. I may still need from time to time to work with Julie or Mark, this is usually the case, to speed things up, and ... " Amos stopped there. It was better to wait until Guy opened up a bit more and divulged what exactly he had on his mind.

Guy tilted his head to one side, waited a few moments, then lifted his head and said " You know that lately we have not had many clients commissioning work, but the markets are now opening up. The little blip of stagnation due to the brief recession seems to be over. I want us to resume in strength and to secure some of the contracts that are being tendered out. There aren't many firms which share our kind of work. I have plans to expand, to attract additional investors, and to, as everyone knows, sell a stake in the company. But that is for later, once we are up and sprinting, and our work commissioning is back to full capacity. I have my eyes on a particular project and my intention is to win that contract. It will be good for our business and for the future survival of the company. "

Guy paused, studying Amos's facial responses and body language. He found none, something he always liked about Amos, for he himself was like that, never divulging exteriorly how and what he was thinking, keeping everyone guessing gave you the advantage and helped you along the way.

" I know your capabilities, and frankly you are the only person in my company who can help pull this off. But I want none of this out, not to anyone. You may elicit some help from Julie or

Mark or whoever, but you stay Stumm. You work on it and you report to me only. What do you say ? "

Amos knew when to spot a one in a life time opportunity, and he straightaway knew this was his big moment and his 'thank your lucky stars chance' for advancement, exactly what the doctor has ordered. And above all, he knew how to handle it, not only in the IT tasks involved, but in working in secrecy. His whole life was a secret to others, he was approachable and yet elusive at the same time, and you could never pin him down on anything. " I am flattered by your confidence and trust in me ", he replied, " and you should never be in a position to regret your decision. "

" Fine, it is all agreed then. Come and see me after lunch, and I shall take you through your assignment. "

Amos liked the project, which Guy explained to him in details. He had heard of Textile Technology, known as TT for short. He had to create an evolving website, normally a very complex task. It would have lots of sites and sites within sites, allowing both customers and administrators a freedom of manoeuvrability and an extreme reach of usage. He was excited by the task ahead, he knew he could do it expertly, and he promised Guy it would be ready by the two months deadline for tendering. Guy took Amos on a couple of meetings with TT for orientation into the company's requirements, and Amos set realising the website in earnest.

Needless to say it was a great success, and his design was preferred to other tenders. It was then announced to the entire staff that they would be working on setting up a complex website for TT that would be taking several months, with the security of running it beyond as it was an evolving website to meet TT's plans for national and hopefully global expansion. The news were received with relief in all quarters, but Angelica was not too pleased to learn that Amos had been the mastermind behind the winning of the contract.

Guy was steaming ahead at full speed, the Company's coffers were filling up, and Guy was resurrecting his desire to sell part or all of his company.

Over the weekend Amos had Valerie for company. He had known her now for some months, and every now and again they would spend some time together. They first met each other at a friend's party, and became intimate friends. Valerie cherished much her liberty and was at heart a feminist. They felt there was common ground in their interests and their inclinations, and this guaranteed a smooth untroubled relationship. That weekend they managed like every time they were together to fill it with various and diverse activities. But Amos's mind was on his bet. He stole many moments to check on the football results. When the first match went his favour he began to dream. And then the next, and the next, all falling neatly into place. He had a full 48 hours before he would know if all ten match results went his way. By Sunday afternoon, seven declared results were a win for his selected teams. The cumulative win was already huge but that was still a far dream. He needed all remaining three wins in his favour. He was getting agitated, and he needed to be by himself, whichever way it turned out to be. He would commiserate or celebrate in solitude. He found an excuse to get rid of Valerie, the pretext that he had some computer work to do before Monday morning which was of the utmost urgency. He sat glued to the television, watching the live results coming through. His heart was missing lots of beats, then it would race fast, and he felt drained. And when it all happened he was overcome with emotions, he collapsed in a heap on the sofa, and burst into tears. They were not the tears he had known as an orphan, wondering why he should be different from all other children, they were the tears of joy, the joy that life is finally smiling on him and good fortune is not deserting him. And he wanted to believe that his heart would now be able to change, would be capable of shedding its grievances against the world, and that he would be able to experience love and compassion.

Monday after work Amos presented himself to the head office of the betting agency and duly collected a cheque for £770,331.00. The agency knew of the existence of a winner, at some considerable loss to them, and they congratulated him. Amos declined publicity. The next morning on his way to work he stopped at the local Barclays Bank with which he had his current account, and deposited the fat cheque. He had to be seen by the bank manager, for they were not accustomed to such vast deposits. And all day at work he kept examining his options.

Chapter 7

Amos rose from his desk and went to sit in one of the two huge armchairs which adorned his large office. He liked sitting there where he found it comfortable, glancing out through the double glass panels of the doors leading to the decorative narrow balcony. He was immersed in deep thoughts. There was something not quite right with the way things were going recently in the company. Guy nowadays came seldom in and relied on Amos to steer the ship. He was always at the end of the phone to Amos when he needed more information or clarifications. He carried his laptop everywhere and could follow what was going on at the click of a button.

Amos could not put his finger on what was nagging at him, and he could not dismiss his worries from the back of his head either. Was this the price one had to pay for being a proprietor, he asked himself. He reassured himself he would get used to it, and would in the long run be able to relax and not get uptight about running the business. He accepted that he needed to keep a close eye on the day to day running of everything, but that this did not mean losing sleep over it. It flowed before when it was not his concern, and would certainly continue to flow now, and there would only be the little snags from time to time as before and which he could sort out easily and simply.

He recalled his bet, his good fortune, and how buying into the company was welcome by Guy. Amos wanted the source of his money kept secret and Guy duly obliged. It was rumoured in the offices that Amos had borrowed a substantial sum of money on a business loan from the bank guaranteed by Guy's share in the company. Angelica and Susanna were up in arms, and maintained they could have done the same, had Guy been truthful about his plans, and that it was unfair not to offer it to them. How naive people could be, thought Amos.

Still he felt uneasy. He rang Julie and asked her to come over to his office. He never stopped admiring this girl, and was making the comparisons with Valerie in his mind when Julie knocked on the door and came in. She wore a lovely blue dress - blue was his colour - and she looked radiant and attractive. He offered her the other armchair.

" Hi Julie. Thanks for coming. How are things with you ? "

" Oh, I'm fine, working on the assignments, quite tricky they are. "

" It is big business for us. We must maintain TT's website and ensure it evolves and keeps pace with their own business. I am told you have some backlog to go through, this is holding work for the others, and ideally you should try to speed up and get to grips with your work load. "

Julie bit her lips. Amos was applying pressure. She thought how much he had changed of late since he bought his 25% share of the company. Whereas before he was always understanding and allowing, offering whatever help she needed, he was now sending ultimatum emails, making extra demands on everyone over and above their endurance, accusing them of laziness, and threatening not to award a pay rise to anyone he considered unproductive.

Julie said " We are all working flat out. The amount of work is overwhelming at present. I presume you want the assignments to be completed at the quality expected. Only last week you burst into our offices complaining of low standards, and now you are asking that we rush the work simply because you have agreed target dates with your client. "

Julie stopped, her eyes welled up with moisture, and her lips were trembling. She went on " How you have changed Amos. I don't think you care how we cope or what we go through. Sometimes I think you have not really changed. May be that is who you really are. Bullying and threatening never lead anywhere, they only create disenchantment and resentment. It looks to me you are in the same league as Angelica, the only difference is that yours is masked. " A couple of tears fell down her left cheek.

Amos did not expect this. Anyone else than Julie and he would have put them in place. Somehow he was weak in front of this vulnerable sensitive and docile girl. He let it pass. " Julie, you misunderstand me and you misunderstand the nature of what we do. We have to deliver on time, and we have to deliver the terms of our contract with TT in terms of quality and quantity. I am not happy that you should get this notion that I am threatening in any way. I am not and will never do. But I have a business to run, and profits to make, otherwise the business may not be viable. Remember that we spend ahead of being reimbursed and there is a limit to how long the company can sustain itself until we are paid our dues. Wipe your tears, will you and get back to work. " He really felt sorry for her. Julie left without looking at him.

He was on the verge of asking her out, but knew it would not be professional. Julie's company was for him a source of freshness and sincerity, and he could do with some right now. He would have to be careful in future and disguise his business and work plans from the staff if he were to gain their confidence.

Amos went home feeling in need of much thinking to do. He now lived in a beautiful four bedroom house in Richmond, owned outright, and felt grateful to his lucky stars for all that. He considered himself secure for life. He was not one to bother with this God idea. For him there was much unknown quantity and much uncertainty in the visible world, let alone in the invisible one. He liked reality, the reality that dealt with our senses, and if one followed the law of the land and did not commit felony then one was in the clear for all post life eventualities. The little things within us that surface as loathing or trickery, these he considered part of our genetic make up and should be tolerated. You fend for yourself, you've got your brains to deal with it, and the law of the land will protect those who could not. The main thing is that you do not break the law.

Amos thought of Mark. He always admired his general flair and his clever reasoning. Mark was a real intellect, You only had to give him the dilemma and he would dissect it to its core components and come up with the solution. Mark saw things differently from everyone else, somehow he was just different, as if his brain had magnifying lenses in its frontal lobe. He noticed all little details and could consequently predict ahead. He always knew what would and what would not work. And he was a connoisseur of people. It must be all that literature stuff he was filling his head with which likely gave him the edge in the way he reasoned, as if he had seen it and experienced it all before.

Amos rang Mark to see if they could meet. Mark was free. Half an hour later they were sitting down to a meal of scampi and chips and a glass of white wine which Amos paid for. He cherished Mark and could count on his friendship. Mark was never a gossiper and everything stayed in his heart and his frontal lobe. This time their talk would not be about play heroines and dissonant symphonies.

" Tell me Mark, do you feel happy at work ? "
Mark fixed Amos and thought this was out of the blue, not the kind of chat he would expect from him. " Something the matter ? " he replied.
" No, it was a general question. I got the impression that there may be some disquiet in the office lately about the tasks allocated to each one of you. " Amos said.
" Do you want a tactful diplomatic answer or the truth ? "
Amos smiled at Mark's ability to describe so much in so few words.
" Just say it in whatever style. "
" I need to know what the problem is first. "
" The problem, Mark, is that there is only one boss and one

steerer to the company, and that is me. It's what I want and what Guy wants that matter, because we know best, our capital is at stake, and to tell you the truth, I do not see why should anyone feel unhappy. "

" What is it that you are trying to achieve ? " retorted Mark. " You want to deliver on your deals with your clients. Fine, that is for the boardroom. We work, each to their role, but pushing through and forcing on us unrealistic additional tasks when it is already so time consuming because of the complexities of their nature and the continuing change in the interface we work on, will not help your case or make us feel appreciated. "

Mark had put it bluntly and in perspective.

" Well, that I accept, but your realism should still make everyone accept that this is the prerogative of business and in the background its share holders, in this instance Guy and me, and that on your part, all of you, you must acknowledge that we work within the accepted framework of labour, a modern, legal, supportive and fair enterprise. "

" This may be true, but how do you measure fairness ? Deep down it is in essence that trustful mutual relationship between proprietor and worker, the appreciation that flows both ways, and that continuous entente through frank and dignified interaction, while at the same time roles and ranks are respected and confirmed. "

Amos did not wish to continue in this debate. Mark had a point. Still, he was uneasy and Mark could sense it.

Suddenly Mark said " I have been meant to tell you, though this is not in my nature, but as I care about the integrity of what we do, that there is some conflict of interest from Angelica's quarter and that you may wish to look into our position with TT. When I was at their head office last week, they made it known that Angelica had been making substantial changes to the designs we supply without discussing it with them first, something they have been unhappy about and which they pointed out has not been conducive to their product output. "

Amos started. This statement from Mark brought it all into focus. So that was it, he thought, the thing that was nagging at him. He relied too much on Angelica, at Guy's insistence, and she was betraying the company, out of malice and out of spite. And he was heading for a show down, the earthquake was gathering pace and would strike anytime now, and he would have to thrash it out with her and with her protégée Susanna.

Amos switched the subject, and he finished off the evening talking with Mark about Bazarov, the immortal character created by Turgenev.

Amos woke up early the next day and prepared himself mentally for the battle ahead. He was at his office before eight. He wanted to go through all TT's documents since they started working on their project. He checked his watch and realised he had been engrossed in the paperwork for over an hour. As he prepared to make his way down the corridor to see Angelica, his phone rang. It was TT's chairman on the other end. Amos made the usual courteous enquiries about the progress of the project and whether everything from his end was in order. Then he listened to the chairman, but what came was definitely not what he expected. He was told directly and without beating about the bush that they were not pleased with the quality of the web page designs, that there were numerous technical problems, that some of the screen functionality was not what they had requested, and that there have been serious snags in the operation of the home page that clients were giving up out of frustration. Moreover he was informed that the operation mode for the shopping cart was defective and with problems around completion of payments.

Amos listened dumbfounded. So it was true, he thought, that his company, always renown for its high quality IT products, had been undermined and compromised. He thanked the chairman and promised to rectify everything at once, and to deliver what had been agreed in their original deal within a few days. What came next was a thunderbolt. The chairman explained that the board of directors had met and had decided to terminate the contract and that they were taking their business elsewhere, and that this was their final decision. He explained that there would not be any entitlement to compensation for lost business as Amos's company had not delivered what had been agreed, and that Textile Technology had actually been losing income as a result of the poor quality of the commodity received.

Amos sank in his armchair. He realised that that was the end. The company had not taken any other projects in order to be able to cope with TT's huge contract. For the first time since landing in this country he had felt despondent, that horrible gnawing feeling he had known before in the orphanage and in the slums of Paris, and which he thought he was rid of for good. And his head was now engaged in the most painful brain storming.

As he sat contemplating his next move, Guy appeared. Amos could see from Guy's look on his face that he had something important to say. He would not just drop in at 9.30 am for a cup of coffee.

' I have to assume that you know the state of affairs our company is in. Has TT chairman spoken to you ? We actually had a long conversation last night and I asked him to ring you as well. Before you say anything, I do not attach any blame to you. I think we bit more than we could chew, and let's face it the staff let us down. May be, just may be you could have spent more time on the floor guiding them, but that is too late now. Anyway, I am selling my share and I have found a buyer. You may wish to stay and be part of the new company, or take the hell out and cash your capital. The opportunities are endless when you have good capital. What do you say? There is no need to rush on your part, but I have been in business for so long and I know when it is time to pull out. "

Without hesitation, Amos said " I am also out. But before that I have one business to conclude. "

He left Guy and went out of his office heading towards Angelica's room.

Amos walked through the ajar door of Angelica's office and took two single steps before stopping, hands in his pockets.
Angelica raised her head and implanted on her face that look of innocent amazement everyone was used to see when she put on the pretence show. " How can I help you Amos ? " she said.
" You can start by explaining what you have been doing regarding the work we have with TT. "
" What? " and then after a brief pause she said " Why exactly did you come into my office ? As you can see I am busy and I have no time for discussions at present. "
" Listen Angelica, and watch my lips carefully. I am your boss, I own part of this company and I pay your wages. So don't delude yourself and think you run this place, because you don't. You get it ! "
" How dare you talk to me like that. The company would be nothing without me. I was here when you were still in your nappies, and I have taught every single person you see around the ins and outs of the business including you. So get out of my office, and when your learn your manners you can come back and tell me what you are after. "
Amos could take it no longer, and he was now shouting his words at Angelica: " You were given clear instructions to produce the designs I have come up with for TT's project and ensure the team followed them meticulously. Instead you got it into your head to change many of the page designs without authority, and the end result of course is a complete disaster and a serious dent to our business and in our client's confidence in our ability to deliver high quality IT configurations. "

Angelica was rattled, and Amos sensed her severe discomfiture. He went on " You know, you have a serious problem, and it is in your head. You delude yourself that you are some kind of rare genius, but the truth Angelica is that your brain lacks that necessary quality that real intellectual people have and that is the ability to create and to formulate. I have watched you over the few years that I have been here, and you were never able to come up with anything realistic or concrete as your own achievement. All you can do is apply what others have designed, and something else which defines your abilities, and that is unless you follow the instruction in the order it is presented you lose your way and you are not able to proceed accurately. And on top of this, you are devious and self centred, and you are willing to stab in the back just to get ahead on others, which I think is a despicable attribute. You are not a team worker, you do not have the good of the company or your colleagues at heart, and your intentions are always doubtful and insincere. "

Amos paused. They were all gathering outside in the corridor, as the shouting had reached them, and they could hear every single word. Angelica screamed back at Amos. " You are an impertinent brute, if anyone is deluded it is you. Get out of my sight, get out of my office. I shall teach you for speaking out of turn. "

Amos fixed her with his gaze for a few more moments, and as he was turning to leave, he said calmly " I would have fired you on the spot, but I leave that joy to the new owner. Guy and I are selling the company this very day. You are a pitiful sight. "

Amos collected his personal belongings from his office and walked out of the building for the last time. Susanna hurried to Angelica's room, shut the door behind her, and they both stayed there longer after everyone else had departed, deliberating and tossing in their heads what is likely to come next. They still felt they were safe, and would carry on in the new company in their respective roles.

The new owner turned up the next day. He had bought the company in its entirety in a matter of hours, after sitting with Guy and Amos, in the presence of each party's respective accountants and solicitors. A week later, Angelica and Susanna received each a letter informing them that the company would no longer be needing their services, and that they would be paid a redundancy lump sum equivalent to five weeks pay. As they left the building after clearing their desks, others commented on how they looked demoralised and ashen white. Nobody felt a great loss at their departure.

Epilogue

Amos retreated to his home in Richmond for a few months. He did not rush into a new adventure and he enjoyed the free time. He paid a visit to Paris. He had fulfilled his ambitions and was left with a substantial capital to invest as he wished. He now works from home on commissions from clients needing IT solutions, and is well known in the market.

Angelica and Susanna have registered with several employment agencies and have both managed to land themselves temporary work from time to time, enough to keep them afloat.

Julie was engaged to be married, and was giving up work altogether. Mark moved on to a hedge fund company, and is learning the trade fast.

Guy had a car accident and broke his spine. He is still recovering in hospital.

The End

THE ASSESSOR

Mr and Mrs Seaman, or Abel and Marina as they are known to their neighbours, live at 15 Seashore Avenue in the village of Waverley, on the outskirts of Seaport Island in the South of England. Abel Seaman retired from his job as a ground worker at the age of sixty having accepted a voluntary redundancy packet from the local council, his employer. He greeted the offer of redundancy with welcome arms, as he felt he had had enough of a working life, and that it was time to reap the benefits of an idle life. Marina, who was one year older than her husband also decided to pack up the part time job she was doing as a shop assistant and retire likewise from all work activity. Abel received an occupational pension straight away, and an attractive redundancy lump sum which he put into a savings account. Five years later he enjoyed receiving his generous state pension, his wife having had hers a year earlier. Abel and Marina lived at their semi-detached house for over thirty years, and the mortgage was paid off five years before. Although their total combined monthly income was a little under sixteen hundred pounds, giving them a reasonably comfortable life, they always believed that they should pounce on any opportunity for free money if the circumstance arose, and they surely kept their eye open on government policies and benefit entitlements in case there was something in it for them.

Abel settled to his daily routine, of waking up at seven in the morning, and going downstairs for a cup of coffee and a quick scan of the news on the television set. He would then go upstairs again with another cup of coffee in hand, this time for his wife who would get out of bed half an hour or so later than her husband after she has sipped her hot drink. They would then engage the bathroom for another hour before they got dressed and headed downstairs for a sit down to breakfast in their modest kitchen. Marina kept a sense of perspective in their home, she had a knack of arranging furniture throughout their home proportionately and with an eye for practicality. The impression you got when you visited them was that of a comprehensively furnished home with all comfort essentials and yet not cluttered in any of its rooms. Late morning they would either stroll to their village centre for a small top-up shopping including the newspapers, and a chat with whomever they are likely to meet of local residents, if the weather permitted to stand for such an activity in the village square, or walk to the water edge to enjoy a sunny day and watch the various birds taking to the air or gliding on the water surface. Twice a week Abel would drive himself and Marina to the nearest supermarket, which happens to be an ASDA store, for a main shopping. Marina would spend time in the afternoon going over her house which she always kept in an immaculate state, something she complimented herself about, while Abel read the newspapers. Then Marina would cook their dinner of the day which they would sit to eat as evening approached. The evening was spent relaxing in the two solid but somewhat worn armchairs in their sitting room, the only reception room they had. Meals were always taken in the kitchen. Abel and Marina did not shy from talking to others, but they never thought of inviting anyone over, and it has been a very long time since anyone had asked them over, a view that was widely circulated that they preferred to keep themselves to themselves.

Life rolled by, Abel and Marina cherished each other's company, and found their idle life a heavenly blessing. Abel never lost his touch when it came to home maintenance, and carried out his duty as a home owner diligently and with a great sense of enjoyment, making sure that the property was always in top shape. Marina supervised the day to day running of their home, which, although it was not elegantly furnished, yet it had all necessary items of furniture, fully functional and fully operational. As responsible homeowners, Abel and Marina Seaman had home insurance, covering contents and buildings. They knew their home contents were not worth much, but at least they were covered for any unfortunate event or calamity not only befalling them but also anyone unlucky enough to suffer an accident or a mishap on their property.

*****

The ironing was done once a week, on Sunday afternoon. Marina preferred to set up the ironing board in the hallway, as it gave her more room to move her arms about in the course of the ironing, and to spread the item of clothing in all directions on and around the board. Abel would carry the board out of the under-stairs cupboard, and spring it open in the middle of the hallway. Marina would set the steam iron upright on the flat square on the right hand side of the ironing board and connect the lead to a socket just above the skirting board. The lead would be away from her working surface, and the position of everything gave her a sense of safety in the way she has planned it and executed it all. Of late Marina was aware that one of the two stands of the ironing board was wobbly and not standing evenly on the carpet. She had drawn Abel's attention to it, and he had looked into it, but had concluded that it was not possible to fix the problem, and that the only solution was to buy a new ironing board, which meant an expense. Marina was not one to throw away appliances unless they had come to their last, and Abel was happy to accept this conclusion, for it meant no unforeseen expenditure. He liked to plan and to keep his outgoings steady and evenly spread over the course of the year.

"I am saving you a purchase of a new ironing board, Darling. Aren't you lucky to have such a non extravagant wife? " said Marina, while ironing one of Abel's shirt. " Imagine if I was one of those women who squander their husband's money without a moment's hesitation, where would we be? " She continued.

" I know, Love " , replied Abel while continuing to read his papers.

" I am careful with this wobbly stand, it's that right side. Anyway, it does the job, and I am happy with it. "

" Good."

" Ironing is very therapeutic darling. You should try it one day. "

" You do a much better job than me, Love. I wouldn't ask you to fix the roof tiles " , interjected Abel.

Suddenly there was a mighty thump.

" Oh no ", cried Marina, " I was dreading this might happen. It's that damn wobbly stand. "

The iron had come off the board and had fallen with a loud thud onto the floor, landing with its hot face down on the carpet.

" How many times I told you to concentrate on your ironing and not get distracted by idle gossip ", shouted Abel from his armchair in the sitting room.

Marina ignored her husband. She never replied when she did not like a comment he made. She bent to her right to pick up the iron from the floor, when to her horror she saw a burnt imprint of the hot iron surface on the carpet, taking a large triangular shape.

" Abel " she now shouted, " come and look at this ".

Abel felt inconvenienced that he should abandon his comfortable slouch in his armchair peering over the newspapers, but if he had learnt one thing in his years of marriage it was that he should never ignore a request from his wife. He got up, turned out of the room and into the hallway to find his wife staring at the floor, clutching her face with both hands, and with a look of horror in her eyes and a gaping mouth. Abel looked where his wife was staring to see a large orange triangle imprint on the carpet.

" What happened ? " he said, but he knew straightaway what had happened. " Oh darling, you should have been careful. "

" You know how careful I am, and always have been. It's that damn wobbly right sided stand, it just like it gave way and the whole iron went toppling over. You must have heard the thud. I could have been burnt " said Marina, raising her voice.

" Thank God you are alright " said Abel, " anyway it is only a damaged bit of the carpet, I am sure we can fix it or spread something over it. "

" Aren't we covered for that sort of mishap ? We are insured aren't we ? We have been forking up every year for that sort of eventuality, so they should replace it or at the very least pay us up to get the carpet replaced. "

Abel's eyes sparkled. He always trusted his wife with her instincts and her planning, for she knew how to handle misgivings and difficulties, and many a time he followed her advice to a successful outcome.

" I shall give them a call tomorrow morning first thing, I shall get the document out right now to see exactly what we are entitled to " Abel said, then he added " let me help you pack up the board. "

" I must finish the ironing, it will not make much difference now, the carpet is ruined anyway. "

Abel continued to talk to his wife as he climbed upstairs to get a look at their insurance policy.
 " Just a thought love, you know our carpet is very worn and not worth much. Do you think this could work against us, the fact that it is so worn that such a burn that has just happened it can be argued that it has not made the carpet that much worse. "

Marina did not like that and she looked up from where she was standing with an expression that said it all. Abel knew that expression well, and actually thought his wife was right in her assessment of the situation. By the time he fished out the insurance policy, his wife had ironed the last item of clothing and was packing away the ironing board in the under-stairs cupboard. She deposited the hot iron on the kitchen surface to allow it to cool down before stowing it away.

Marina looked on as Abel spread the insurance policy document on the kitchen table, and there in clause 5, they were surely covered for accidental damage, again something his wife has insisted upon when they took out their policy.

" Good " said Abel, " we're on, it appears we are well covered.
"

" You phone them tomorrow when they open, and see if you need to fill a form. May be they do it all over the phone " said his wife. " You know what to say, don't you " she continued.

" I know " replied Abel. He did not see any difficulty handling this affair, and he settled himself in his armchair, opening a can of beer to unwind, after he prepared a small glass of sherry for his wife, her favourite relaxation drink. She was already dreaming of changing the whole carpet in the hallway, and thinking how fortunate perhaps it has been for this accident to happen as she had been wanting to change this old tired carpet for so long. She even dreamt in her sleep of walking over a new carpet, velvety in touch and velvety in colour. Abel had no apprehension at all about sorting this out the next day as he drifted to sleep.

*****

Abel woke up the next morning at seven as was his custom. He went downstairs for his cup of coffee and a scan of the morning news on the television set. He brought upstairs a cup of coffee for his wife as was the custom. They both followed their daily routine, and went about their morning as usual for everyday. Anyone seeing them would have thought the day was like any other day, with nothing to worry about and nothing that needs some prioritising. On the surface they looked calm, but deep down in their minds, there was the most engaging activity. Today was like no other day, for since their retirement they had not come across any new event that needed additional effort or extra thinking on their behalf. Today, they felt, there was something that had to be done and achieved, and that created some sort of mental strain they had not come to experience since their retirement. Once showered and dressed Abel sat at the kitchen table, ready for the task ahead. He had left the insurance document spread open on the table from the night before, and could with a wink of an eye locate the insurers telephone number, the policy number and the important clause 5. Marina, not wanting to unsettle her husband, stayed out of the kitchen, but nearby enough to follow the developments and to ensure they unfolded as they should, ready to step in if this became necessary.

Abel rang the number on the document, and went through a series of options before he was ultimately connected to an attractive female voice introducing herself as Vanessa and asking if she could be of any help. Mr Abel, calmly, explained that they had an insurance policy for home contents that included accidental damage, and that the evening before the hot iron had accidentally toppled from the ironing board and landed on the carpet in the hallway causing a massive burn to the carpet, and that as such they have come to realise that the fitted carpet would have to be replaced for new if they were lucky enough to find a match in colour, otherwise likely a whole new fitted carpet for the hallway. He managed to
utter all this out in one go, trying to sound concerned but at the same time rational and pragmatic, which he had rehearsed

the previous night as he lay in bed to sleep and the couple of times he woke up during the night. Marina looked pleased with her husband's performance. Vanessa, at the other end, was silent for a few seconds then asked for the insurance policy number.
" Bear with me a moment, Mr Seaman, is that correct, while I locate your policy " Vanessa interjected, then after a few moments " Could you confirm your full name please and the first line of your address ". Abel obliged her.
" For the purpose of security could you also confirm your date of birth Mr seaman " she went on. Abel again obliged her with the information. " I shall have to put you on hold while I check the details of your policy Mr Seaman ", and suddenly Abel found himself listening to some music which he found irritating and monotonous. He covered the mouthpiece of the phone, and spoke loud for his wife to hear " Why do they always put on this boring classical music, what is wrong with songs like I will survive or Love me love me do ? ". He found the music too loud and kept the phone a little away from his ear, for what felt like eternity.
Vanessa came back on the line and said
" Thank you for holding. One of our assessors will be visiting you this afternoon to assess the damage and to advise the company. Will someone be at home ? "
" We are not going anywhere, so your assessor should find us in and we look forward to their visit " replied Abel.
" OK then. If you have any other queries you can ring us on the same number. Can I help you with anything else Mr Seaman ? " said Vanessa.
" No " replied Abel, " you have been very helpful thank you, bye bye ".

Abel hung up and came out of the kitchen looking for his wife and saying " They are sending an assessor to assess the damage ".
" I already heard you darling " replied Marina, " I guess that's what insurers do, but they will not cut us down, we will be cleverer and insist on our full right. "

" Of course " came the reply.

Abel and marina occupied themselves in the morning with various home chores. They stayed clear of the hallway carpet and did not even apply the vacuum cleaner to it, as they wanted the carpet to look as orange as possible, to highlight the severe damage that has been done, which in their view is not amenable to any form of cleaning. They realised that the carpet was not burnt through where the iron had landed, but they had already made up their minds that they would be getting a new carpet replacement, likely a totally different texture and colour shade and as such a whole new fitted carpet for the entire hallway to avoid disharmony and unsightliness. After lunch, they sat in their respective armchairs not particularly doing anything special but waiting anxiously for the assessor to make their appearance.

*****

The afternoon dragged on and Abel and Marina were beginning to doubt if the so called assessor was ever going to come, when suddenly they heard the door bell. Abel went to answer the door with Marina at his tail. When Abel opened the door he was greeted by a short stout man with a large bald in the middle of his head and a bulging belly hanging out of his trousers belt. He was carrying a little black cloth bag under his left arm. Abel scanned quickly the human specimen standing in front of him, the bushy eyebrows, the open necked white shirt, and the small ears hidden behind thick black side whiskers.

" Mr Seaman ? inquired the man.

" Yes " said Abel.

" I am Tom Cleverly, the assessor from Fair & Square Insurance. I have come to look at your damaged carpet. "

" Do come in " said Abel, and stepped aside to let Mr Cleverly through, and as he stepped into the hallway it was Marina's turn to give him a full head to toe examination.

Marina offered to make Mr Cleverly a drink but he declined saying with a broad smile
" That is very kind of you Mrs Seaman, but I would rather not thank you, as I do not want to be caught short as I have been travelling all day and I have still got two more home visits to make before I head back to the office. Would it be possible to have a look at the carpet ? "

" It is under your feet " said Abel.
The hallway was not a big space by normal standards and so Mr Cleverly happened to have stepped over it as he made his way into their home. He immediately looked down and saw half a yard away a large orange triangular iron imprint.

" Oh " he said, " I see, it is not very much, but there is some damage. "

" What do you mean - not very much ! " said Marina. She did not like that at all. " This burnt piece of the carpet will not last, it is likely it will make a big hole in no time at all, and what would visitors say when they see such monstrosity. "

Mr Cleverly knew from experience of dealing with women like Mrs Seaman, that the best way forward is not to antagonise but to agree and steer the person somehow to where he wants to end up.

" Oh Mrs Seaman, I totally agree, this is a monstrosity. I was only referring to the actual size of the damaged carpet, to try and see what we can offer you, and … "

Mr Cleverly stopped talking and looked again at the carpet and then at Mr Seaman this time, trying to gage the situation and whether Mr Seaman was of the same view as his wife or more malleable and more realistic.

All three were standing in the hallway in almost a full circle staring at the orange imprint on the carpet which was now in their middle.

" May I ask you Mr Cleverly what is your role exactly in all this ? " suddenly said Abel.

" Please call me Tom ", said Mr Cleverly with a big grin, " I am a qualified assessor ".

" And what's that, Tom ? " said Abel.

" I assess, I am a functional assessor, which means I assess functionality. "

" Functionality ! " came in Marina.

" Yes, I assess function of the item in question. For example, looking at your carpet, I know what its function is when undamaged, having seen your hallway and heard from you about your expectations, and then I have to assess the impact the damage has done to the previous status quo, having inspected first the actual damage and assessed the resulting loss of function so to speak ", replied Tom while drawing in the air with both his indices the apostrophe sign.

" Isn't that just a matter of opinion ? After all one may disagree, and then we have a difference of opinion, the way you look at it that is different from our expectation, which is bound to happen, not just because you represent the interest of your company, but more importantly the lack of objectivity which is likely to cause unhappiness and grievance. Do we have to agree with what you say or decide ? "

Marina felt very proud of her husband at that moment. She was glad she was present, and thought to herself that her presence must have given him the courage to stick to his guns.

" Let me explain ", said Tom, " Insurers have long ago consulted each other and have come up with a universal agreement and universal methods and compensations to be adopted by all of them, for the purpose of fairness and objectivity, as you have just pointed out Mr Seaman, and they abide by a code which we, assessors apply in the field. "

Tom was trying to win them on his side, and avoid any sense of confrontation. He was aware that the damage to the carpet was insignificant in terms of monetary compensation, and therefore to pre-empt any headaches to himself and to the company he had already made up his mind to let it be, but the question was how far should he go. He also wanted to stay in control, and to maintain a certain degree of tension in his dealings with the elderly couple, which he knew was crucial to staying on top. And so he decided to lay his credentials and his authority.

" I am a collegiate assessor. "

" What ? said both Abel and Marina in one voice.

" I am a collegiate assessor. That is my qualification. To be a collegiate assessor I had to undertake training organised by the company over three days, and pass a test at the end. "

" You mean you sat an exam. " said Abel.

" Sort of " replied Tom, " I had to pass a multiple choice questionnaire of ten questions covering the whole syllabus of insurance, and get all answers correctly. That's quite tough you know, but I did. This was a few years ago. I am a registered collegiate assessor ", continued Tom, brimming with confidence bordering on the arrogance.

" Listen Tom " said Abel, " with all due respect, that is a matter for you and we do not understand it, what we want to know now is whether you are prepared to authorise a new carpet for the whole hallway, given the damage and the likelihood that we will not find a match to patch it up. "

Tom was getting a little irritated that they were trying to snatch control from him, and he felt he should check them in place even though he was acquiescing to their demands, and decided it was time they knew that their carpet was extremely worn and useless, that he knew they were exaggerating its value, and that they were in essence mercenaries and profiteers except that he did not say it quite bluntly but made an inference nonetheless.

Tom witnessed the drama unfolding, he knew what was coming like the back of his hand, he was used to it, and had lost count of the number of times he had seen it acted in front of him. Marina was now tearful, Abel had his arms round her comforting her, she was mumbling how dare he thinks this of them, that they were victims, that life was tough for them, that there was no fairness or empathy in the world they lived in, and that they would have to complain and take the matter onwards to the ombudsman. Abel admonished Tom for his behaviour and lack of sensitivity, threatened he would complain to the highest authority, and that Tom would live to regret it that the had upset his wife so gravely. She would now be ill for several days, he said, and that he would hold Tom personally responsible for this.

Having done the dirty deed which he always found a little uplifting to his morale in such situations, something he did from time to time to venture his frustration, he became all sweet again, and said slowly and clearly, through Marina's

tears and Abel's remonstrances, ensuring that they heard him well
" Oh I am sorry Mrs Seaman, Mr Seaman, that is not my intention at all, I was just pointing out the full picture, after all I have to provide a factual report to my company, but I have the discretion to grant you your wish, it is fair that you should get a full compensation, and I am recommending a full new carpet of your choice for the hallway, and the company will surely endorse my recommendation, they are not known to go against our advice. You should get a letter of confirmation to that effect within the week. '

From the state of despair, suddenly Marina's face shone with delight, and her demeanour changed from one of quasi-despondency to sheer ecstasy. She almost jumped for joy. Abel looked ten years younger at this news and seemed to forget his arthritic knees, moving so lightly on his legs that even his wife was so impressed.

Tom shook hands with both of them, and hurried out of the house, reflecting on another success story, which depended on the perspective one adopted in the case and there were many. He was aware that in the insurance business it was all squares and roundabouts, customers paying for customers, all in their turn, and profits were still made.

*****

Three days later, Abel and Marina received the following letter from Fair & Square insurance.

Mr & Mrs Seaman
15 Seashore Avenue
Waverley
Seaport Island

Dear Mr and Mrs Seaman

Following the visit to your premises by our capable qualified collegiate assessor Tom Cleverly, I am delighted to offer you a cheque for the sum of £300.00 as compensation for your damaged hallway carpet, on the basis of like for like, to be used at your discretion. We hope this will meet with your acceptance, and I take this opportunity to thank you for your continuing custom.
Yours sincerely

Tom Mouseley
Director of Functional Assessments

Abel looked at Marina with a sheepish smile. Marina shrugged her shoulders and said " The least they could do. Anyway the carpet does not look that bad at present, we can save that money away, don't you think? "

Abel kept smiling, this time with contentment, put his head in his newspapers and continued reading. Marina headed for the kitchen with a sense of satisfaction and job well done.

****

MY CLOSE FRIEND

My Close Friend - A chronicle

8 October 2015

I am delighted for a close friend of mine who has now left Siberia after thirteen years of incarceration, for highlighting the authorities failing systems, their incompetent management and their illogical policies. He has reached St Petersburg and has taken up residence on Nevsky Prospekt. He intends to write his memoirs and is enlisting my help.

Right now he is sitting in Cafe Zinger overlooking Kazan Cathedral where he attended mass this morning. He has sent me a selfie. Good on you Boris Mikhailich Warovsky. I am thrilled for your regained freedom. Your flair and inspiration will be missed in Siberia.

I can hear you whistling the tune 'You never know what you've got till it's gone baby'.

***

19 October 2015

I talked to Boris Mikhailich Warovsky the other day via video link. Since leaving Siberia he has been enjoying himself out and about in St Petersburg. He told me a funny story about a letter he received a few days after fleeing and heading west. As I have told you before he has taken up residence in a beautiful apartment on Nevsky Prospekt. He goes down every morning and sits in Cafe Zinger overlooking Kazan Cathedral, and enjoys a healthy seedy bread sandwich of salmon and crème fraîche over a cup of strong coffee with hot milk. He takes with him his organiser and plans the day ahead, meeting good and interesting people and visiting attractive and mind stimulating places. He cannot get over the fact that everything and everywhere feels fresh and exhilarating. Anyway, going back to the letter, a few days ago the postman delivered this strange official looking letter. Boris realised where it could have come from, and thought to himself O-O ! He told me that it did not trouble him in the least to open it as he expected the usual official non-sense, perhaps to confirm that he has truly left Siberia, the kind of thing an Intellectual from St Petersburg would call ' Official Remorse after the Event '. He opened it with a sense of victory and amusement to read the following:

" Dear Mr Warosvky
I am writing to inform you that following your departure from our miserable camp in Tiskhaltoba in Siberia you are advised that you are being stripped of your rights to be treated as a resident offender in the whole region, which it has always been considered a privilege bestowed on our detainees. Moreover we forbid you to engage in hard labour anywhere else on the planet particularly if it resembles in any way the hard labour we inflict on our lost for ever prisoners. I take this opportunity in wishing you happiness and total freedom, something we consider unbecoming and adverse in our idealistic environment. Any helpful thoughts you may harbour on this matter will not be approved by our authority and will be contested and revoked.
Your devoted Commandant
Darius Wagorin Pavlovich "

Boris was chuckling as he recounted this hilarious affair, and I could not stop myself from sharing his chuckles. We parted electronically, for he was getting on with his inspiring activities, and I reflected on how some 'Siberian' people on this earth seem to be enveloped in a thick fog of their own unaware that there is a wide world out there more interesting and more intelligent, and that they seem to live in a warp they cannot escape from due to their irrational, static and bird-size lump of grey cells.

***

1 November 2015

You will all remember my friend Boris Mikhailich Warovsky who was incarcerated in Siberia for thirteen years. I told you before how he settled nicely in St Petersburg, enjoying his regained freedom. You will remember the strange letter he received from the Siberian authorities a few days after departing. Anyway, I am sure you all remember what I have related concerning my dear friend Boris. I have been in contact with him on a weekly basis. He has been travelling around, and visiting very interesting places such as palatial homes and art galleries. He has also been invited to many sought after galas, and I am actually very pleased for him.

Anyway, we both agreed it was time to see each other again after such a long time, and we decided to meet up midway, in Kraków. I checked in at The Kossacks Hotel overlooking the river Wisla. Boris stayed at Copernicus Hotel. You know of course that Corpernicus, the first to state that the earth was round, was Polish. Boris and I agreed to meet in the Main Market Square opposite the Cloth Hall in the old town. We were both ecstatic when we met, and any onlooker could have glimpsed the happiness radiating in our faces. We entered St Mary's Basilica and knelt in front of the Holy Sacrament to give thanks for the good things despite all that Boris had been through. We sat afterwards for a glass of beer and a plate of bigos, the traditional meat and cabbage dish.

Over the meal, Boris said to me:
" You know my friend, I rarely now think of where I was only a few months ago, and of the last thirteen years, but when occasionally the thought crosses my mind, all I feel is contempt for those who governed over us, the same contempt I had for them when I was in. For you see Jean-Pierre (that is my name), fools are cowards and cowards are fools. But then smaller worlds prefer fools, and it is where integrity evaporates and instead cowardice reigns, and cowardice breeds more cowardice, that eventually these small people start to believe they are the heroes and the saviours, suffering from derealisation, and believing all the while that the injustice they inflict is the truth and the perfect ideal. But you could feel it in your bones how these people were always realising they were on shaky grounds, they needed to continuously submit and degrade others to make themselves feel they are on the right track, that what they have come up with is the right thing, and that they must reign supreme for they are always right in their assessment and their verdict. I could not even convince myself they were poor souls, for in all reality they were deluded individuals seeking to justify their methods through your willingness to submit, and boy o boy, prisoners did submit for they had no hope in hell in leaving the place even if they had the opportunity to escape, for Siberia is half the earth away from what they knew before and they would not have been able to realise the transition or fend for themselves, that deep was their entrenchment in their miserable existence. Our immediate goaler, the one assigned to our territory was called Zusanna Homerovna Lickamanov, uncleverly devious and shut in in her tiny vulgar world. She could not tolerate any discourse or dialogue, it destroyed her, for she was never able to grasp the gist of the discussion in hand or formulate a reasonable reply. She would shout at you and run away only to return with a buddy or a helper and then engage in a tirade of intimidation to

regain the upper hand she had earlier lost intellectually. Integrity is a rare commodity Jean-Pierre, it is what makes the individual who has it stand out clearly from the herd, and it gives that individual that subtle power which the others can perceive and fret over but are unable to defeat. One day I faced Zusanna and said to her ' Why do you do this ? '. Do you know what she said? ' May be you get too clever and they ditch me and have you instead running this place. ' Can you believe it! She actually thought in her small brain that I, a prisoner, could be promoted to run the camp. Now you can have an idea of the quality of the echelon of workers who ran the prison camp. My dear Jean-Pierre, fools are cowards and cowards are fools.

Boris paused, took another mouthful of bigos followed by some beer and continued " I did not tell you that I have found a part time job as a senior clerk at the Admiralty. I oversee a dozen of petty officials. The hours are short and the work is light. "

" I am really delighted for you Boris " I said.

We spent the day together, we visited a few more churches, and we climbed Wavel Hill. We dined in the evening in an elegant restaurant on the main square. Time flew, and next morning we made our way to the airport, for the return flight to our respective countries.

In the days that followed I often reflected on what Boris said, and I felt myself the same contempt for those people Boris dealt with and for all people who are similarly stuck in that absurd fanciful world, a world bent on cruelty and injustice.

*****

15 November 2015

As I have told you before, I am always in contact with my friend Boris, practically on a weekly basis. We talk to each other via video link. St Petersburg is three hours ahead in time, and it was not yet 6 am this morning when Boris rang me on my tablet. Boris was all excitement and chuckling in his usual manner.

" Hey, Jean Pierre, are you awake ? "

" What's up Boris ? " I replied, rubbing my eyes, and trying to concentrate on the face grinning from the screen in front of me.

" Jean Pierre, you look exactly the same waking up in your pyjamas as when I meet you during the day. How do you manage it ? "

" It's God's Grace, Boris, for those good people who mean no harm to others. "

" I am one of them then ", replied Boris, " my gaoler Zusanna always said to me I looked no different when cutting stone than when I got up in the morning. Hey, you and I are the good guys. " And he chuckled loudly.

I like Boris when he chuckles like that. The guy has a heart of gold. His thirteen years in Siberia did not change his flair or his warm and attractive manner. " So what's up ? " I said.

" I received another letter this morning. "

" Not again. " I said.

" Listen to what it says. It is hilarious Jean Pierre. These guys are truly lost souls. The letter is signed by the same Commandant. "

And he read the following to me:

" Dear Mr Warovsky

I write to you in my official capacity as the commandant of the ' lost for ever ' camp. I realise, to my chagrin, that you are one of the exceptions who have managed to extricate themselves from our community of hard labour to live in your previous refined, easy going, highly intellectual and free world, which I consider a setback. I am aware that this has created for us a real dilemma, as many of our prisoners are thinking along those lines. I have had to give an account to the Siberian authorities, and we have identified individuals within the camp administration whose actions have led to this unfortunate and quite damaging for us affair. I believe they were punishing prisoners for cutting stones too thin or too wide, too small or too large, too long or too short, too rough or too smooth. The authorities have now demoted those individuals from the role of running the prisoners to prisoners themselves. This should not come as a surprise, for we consider everyone an offender but at times we give a reprieve from the duties of an offender, but that does not mean it is a permanent dispensation. You will recall some of these names who have now been demoted; Markovich, Aliovna, Amanovna, Mikhailich, Kangidich.

Though here in Siberia we always convince ourselves that our conscience is clear, nevertheless your departure has filled us with a sense of uneasiness as it has ripped through the illusion that we have for so long managed to preserve. We have consulted the goblins - you were the first to remark on the flimsiness of our system and on its futility - and the consensus has been, and I want you to note this word carefully for it is the foundation of everything we do, that we should, as an act of contrition and reparation, offer you the sum of 80000 roubles as a modest compensation for what we have tried to inflict on your intellect unsuccessfully.

I hope I shall never be asked or be in a position to write to you again, for it fills me with a desire to follow in your footsteps which my convictions prevent me from doing.

I wish you resentment, unhappiness and failure, which I know will never happen to you.

Your Commandant

Darius Wagorin Pavlovich

" Ho, Ho, Boris, that is hilarious " I said. " 80000 roubles is the equivalent of £1600. Any plans for this landed fortune ? Ha, Ha, Ha. " I could not stop laughing.

Boris was still chuckling. " I am inviting many of my old friends to watch Rossini's opera William Tell, and I have reserved a ticket for you. It is performed at the Marinsky theatre in St Petersburg. I really hope you make it. Afterwards we shall retire to Cafe Zinger for the debate. Ha, Ha, Ha. "

I said good bye to Boris, and lay down in bed again, for an extra hour of sleep. As I drifted off I thought of William Tell fighting the Austrian occupation of his beloved country, eventually to conquer and restore freedom.

*****

5 December 2015

Boris made a surprise visit to London this weekend. We both attended the same conference on the science of reliability. Both of us found it very informative and I asked him what attracted him to this subject. I thought may be his new job in the Admiralty in St Petersburg required a certain degree of discipline and hence reliability. For me it was just another opportunity to listen to the learned and the knowledgeable. I expected Boris to chuckle hearing my question and he did not disappoint. We had already strolled down Regent Street, which was closed to traffic with pedestrians capitalising on its full width, among the throngs of people enjoying London on a cold but crisp evening, and we halted frequently to look at the shop windows which displayed animated scenes and dazzling lights. Above us, stretching from one roof to the other across the street hung various attractive luminous festive shapes. " I have never seen such huge crowds before in London. " said Boris.

We eventually reached Fortnum & Mason, and after roaming round the store taking in the beautiful array of the sweets merchandise, we sat down to champagne dinner. When we finished and over coffee Boris suddenly exclaimed
" I shall answer your question about why I chose to attend this conference ".
I had forgotten about it, having despaired at receiving an answer earlier. Knowing Boris well, sometimes he prefers to keep his thoughts and his feelings bent up within him, fearful that listeners may not fully appreciate what he has to say or relate. But Boris always trusted me.
" I shall tell you another funny Siberian story, Jean Pierre, if you want to call it that way, but it is actually dead serious. " He hesitated for a brief moment before continuing.

" I was cutting stone ..... I was cutting stone day in day out. That is all I ever did. They checked what each prisoner produced on the day, and they always checked the quality of the stones. I was never able to comprehend this. It was making a thing out of no entity, creating an illusion that quality was at stake, when in actual fact the whole purpose of the exercise was to simply cut stone. Moreover the stone that we dealt with could not have had any commercial value or use, because it came from useless quarry. The prisoners did not give the matter any thought, seeing perhaps that this was another reason to keep the guards busy and pompous, until one day, on our morning assembly, we were informed that from then on a new system was to be introduced, allowing for variability of the stone. Imagine what went through my mind. I knew things would not be the same any longer, and that harsher days lay ahead. These people are ignorant, Jean Pierre, they have never been exposed to challenging intellect. You and I know, that to achieve quality, you need to keep the unwanted variability to a minimum. How then were we to address absurd variabilities like the appearance of the stone, its shape, its texture, its size, its solidity, and whatever else, for the list was increasing by the day. And then talking about the way you cut each stone, how you present the cut stones, etc., was becoming foolish, absurd and immaterial. I took it on me to tell it to them straight, and I did so on more than one occasion, but this led to increasing my stone cutting load out of spite. And then came the final crunch for me. We were told on another day in no uncertain terms that we now had to have our practice of cutting stone recorded on video, and that each one of us will have a microphone attached to our overall every morning when we set off to labour, the purpose of all this was to monitor our behaviour and what we say and do, to be used against us when the authorities were not satisfied with our stone cutting, the punishment for which is one-day-meal less and open humiliation in the morning assembly, in addition to even closer monitoring and greater labour burden.

The interesting thing about our sentence in Siberia is that it is not binding. This may seem odd to you, but in being shipped over it was made clear that in as much as the authorities reserved the right to increase the length of your sentence for any dissent, the prisoner had a way out if they could fix it all up themselves and manage the self ejection out and the journey back to the real world. So I invoked my perdition (to them) and my salvation (to me), and here I am, looking into the reliability science, that deliberate decision to vary our usual life which is very different from variation due to failure and unreliability. "

Boris winked at me, and I understood at that moment exactly the argument this real gentleman was trying to make. I smiled back at him, and we said no more on the subject except perhaps to agree that it would be extremely useful for the Siberian authorities to send those wretched supervisors on a course in the study and practice of improving improvement !

It was time for me to drive back south, and I took my leave from Boris who headed back to his hotel in Mayfair. He was flying to St Petersburg the next day.

*****

12 March 2016

I am in St Petersburg. I arrived here a week ago and I have been staying at Petro Palace Hotel right in the city centre. As you come out of the entrance, there in front of you on the opposite side of the wide road is where Tchaikovsky used to live. There is a plaque on the building wall marking his name. A few metres to the right of the hotel entrance is where Gogol had his apartment, and there is a plaque marking the place. Round the corner from where Tchaikovsky resided I was told by a passer-by - who stopped when he saw me taking photos of Tchaikovsky's apartment balcony on the first floor, and who insisted I should follow him to the next building - that a great commandant by the name of Estefan Pavlovich had his home there. I wondered, as the man was gesticulating with his arms and frothing at the mouth as he spoke, if the said commandant was not related to Darius Wagorin Pavlovich, the commandant who oversaw the Siberian camp where my friend Boris was incarcerated for thirteen years.

As you walk to the right you come across Nevsky Prospekt in a matter of moments, and crossing the road at the main junction you glimpse the Hermitage about 200 metres away in all its magnificence, and all you had to do to reach it is to cross the elegant Palace Square dominated by Alexander Column, leaving to your south the General Staff Headquarters. This square has been the setting of many dramatic effects and the famous storming of the Winter Palace. The column commemorated Tsar Alexander I's victory over Napoleon. To the left of the hotel you get a good view of the golden dome of St Isaac's Cathedral.

You will remember that Boris had invited me to attend Rossini's opera William Tell at the Marisnky Theatre on the occasion of the compensation he received from the authorities following his release. We saw the performance two evenings ago, and some of Boris's trusted friends were also invited. Prior to the opera we had dined at a nearby lavish restaurant, and it was my first taste of Russian cuisine which I found exotic and exhilarating. I tucked into all four courses with relish and great appetite, and I found Russian Champagne and wine to my great liking. Russians know how to dine in the same way as they know how to love and how to have fun. I judged the opera production to be a great success, and you can never tire of watching William Tell on stage, where you empathise with the Swiss uprise under his leadership to overcome the tyrant rule by their neighbour the Austrians. It is a gripping story, and when Tell stood to aim his arrow at the apple balanced above his son's head you could hear a pin drop, despite the counterpointing music running in the background.

During the past week I made it a must to visit Peterhof, but my greatest enjoyment has been promenading up and down Nevsky Prospekt and stopping at the rich and magnificent Kazan cathedral for a prayer, or for afternoon tea at Cafe Zinger. I strolled many a time along Griboyedov Canal all the way to the onion-domed Church of the Resurrection, admiring the beautiful architecture on either side of the canal as I went along.

I saw Boris a few times during the past week, and on one of these occasions it was only the two of us. Boris was itching to tell me about the Siberian camp. He had more news to convey and I was a little surprised that such news could still reach him. I knew he was not in touch or even thought about the past. Boris himself told me so over a glass of Mukuzani red wine.
" You know Jean Pierre ", he said, " the time that I spent in Siberia seems a long way in the past, and I am not one to dwell on the past, but when news reach me inadvertently, and the news describes chaos and bleak conditions, I cannot stop myself laughing and gloating. "

And Boris chuckled, his usual chuckle, when his eyes seem brighter and his face animated, and to tell you the truth, I was simply waiting to hear him chuckle, one of the many things I love about my friend.

" So what's up this time? ' I asked.

" Oh, wait till you hear this ", came the reply. " The commandant Darius Wagorin Pavlovich took it upon himself to introduce the measure of reliability in the stone cutting by the prisoners, while at the same time observing the variability of the presenting stone. He seems to have invented a whole new science, for he wanted the prisoners to cut stone according to set parameters while at the same time coping with the variety of stone they come face to face with everyday. This man has been changing the rules governing the camp practically every few days, whimsically and out of boredom I suspect, and he comes up with absurd notions and doomed activities, which by the way he calls enterprises as if prisoners cutting unwanted stone was the epitome of modern civilisation, while sitting in his shack behind a large decayed desk sifting through endless useless papers and insisting all the while that this was a worthwhile enterprise for the good of the prisoners not just in the present but also for the future generations. "

Boris paused, chuckled, sipped from his wine glass, and resumed his discourse. " One of the prisoners I befriended when I was in, a young man named Kiryakich, became the target of the supervisors, on the basis that he was not able to tackle the stone variability and produce a reliable end product cutting. I got on well with Kiryakich, he is a peaceful accommodating fellow, but he was so bullied - as you know in every community the majority would always pick on the person who is either weak or perceived as not fitting within that community - that he began to suffer nightmares and severe phobia of simply being around the quarry, and he became ill, vomiting one day, fainting on the other, complaining of headaches or blurred vision, losing his balance or feeling his legs giving way underneath him. What do you think happened to him? '

' He would have ben tortured, I should think ! The system never allows dissent, whatever the reasons ", I said.

" Oh no, the commandant concluded that Kyriakich was no good after all, as he could not supply them with cut stone, and they decided he should leave the camp with immediate effect, as if the unwanted and good for nothing end product itself was more important than the state of being a prisoner in hard labour cutting stone day after day. "

" Where is Kyriakich now? "

" Kyriakich is now back in Segiyev Posad, his home town. It is about 75 km from Moscow, heading northeast. "

" Good for him ", I said.

" Definitely good for him ", came the reply, " and moreover, I have learnt that he has also been paid a modest compensation for lasting four years on the site. These people are fools, Jean Pierre. They drive away the very prisoners they incarcerate, actually they let them leave when they can no longer be bullied into doing what they bully them for. I told you before that being sent to Siberia does not prevent the individual opting out if they can manage to arrange it for themselves. Usually the prisoner insubordinates, and either the authorities relent or the prisoner is chucked out. "

I found it very interesting to hear all this, and now I had a very good picture of that Siberian environment. I reminded Boris what he had told me on our previous encounter that the supervisors were turned into quasi prisoners, joining their captives in their hard labour.

Boris's eyes sparkled again and he said " That is very true. There is even worse. I heard that the Commandant, no longer happy in his post, had decided to move on and rejoin the military establishment in the capital. He has been allocated a role of overseeing all the paperwork that is received from the camp concerning prisoners and staff, and reaching a decision on whether to advise ejection or transfer, an activity that everyone knows is idiotic and dead end. "

During the rest of the evening we talked about world economy, Tolstoy, Christian faith, and Donizetti. I should see Boris this evening, I have invited him to dine with me in the hotel restaurant. I have reserved a bottle of Tsinandali, a refreshing dry white, to compliment our meal. I must tell you that I have found Russian beer quite appealing. St Petersburg is the capital of Russian beer. I fly home tomorrow, for all good things must always come to an end. I like Russia, its rich history, its rich literature, and its magnificent heritage.

****

James and the Little Mermaid

James Fletcher worked for Solomon & Solomon, Hedge Funds specialists right in the heart of the financial district in London. He was thirty-one years old, still single, and lived in a small detached house in St John's Wood in the north of the city. Physically, he was an average height for a man, had managed to keep a desirable weight avoiding a paunch, and still had all his scalp hair about him. His face was manly enough but his features were those of a cute and handsome boy. His colleagues and friends had always commented on how younger than his age he looked, with not the slightest sign of an impending butterfly at the temple. James's eyes were olive green, which accentuated the beauty of his face. His nose and his forehead had roman physiognomy, his ears were delicate in their size and shape, and his lips were full and well defined. You could see his Adam's apple whenever he wore an open-necked shirt. And you would have been able to glimpse his well proportioned collar bones, which imparted the illusion of broad shoulders. And if you met him, you would be bowled over by his sartorial dress sense. He wore matching colours, graded from top to bottom or from bottom to top, avoiding stark contrast of colours, and though his clothes might have been referred to as plain, he was able to combine them in a way that was attractive and delightful.

James got on well with everyone at the office. He was diligent at his work, and was popular with everyone. He was highly regarded by his superiors, and was very experienced in investment banking. He was also popular on the social scene, and many a girl desired him as the ideal partner and future husband. James had had his share of girlfriends, but none of the relationships led anywhere. Not that any ended in discord, on the contrary, it only faded away as he felt it was not what he was looking for. He was a pure romantic at heart, and had been dreaming of the girl who would capture it. He dreamt her as having an angelic face, soft attractive eyes, long chestnut hair, delicate skin and dainty hands, and he dreamt the way he wanted her to gaze at him, to tilt her head to one side with bursting femininity, and to smile showing beautiful little dimples. He dreamt her with a girlish figure, a soft voice, a sensitive soul and an intelligent mind. And he dreamt how they would be so identical, mirroring each other, understanding each other without the need to say much, and loving her and being loved by her with spontaneity and devotion. It had not happened yet and he often wondered whether he would ever meet her or how long he would have to wait. He knew she was out there, but he needed all the providence to let their paths cross each other at the right time and without delay before obstacles would by then have stood in their way.

One day at the end of March James was called to see the senior manager in charge of the office who informed him that there would be a client exchange with the Stock Exchange in Copenhagen known as the Borsen. They needed someone over there to oversee future commodity activities in amber gem, which is actually brought over from the southern Baltic, but which Denmark has some monopoly over, and where jewellery is then made out of the fossil resin. James listened to his manager telling him how they think he is the right man for this enterprise which is for a period of six months, as he is familiar with Eastern European markets, and would be instrumental in helping Solomon & Solomon to set up lucrative derivative funds that are likely to be very popular with their own clients and which should prop up their trading activities and bids.

James was given one week to prepare. He was told that accommodation would be arranged for him close to his place of work and that he would be met on arrival and helped to settle in. He was also told that his flight had already been booked, a club class seat on British Airways with entitlement to forty kilograms in weight for luggage. James did not think he would be worse off going to Copenhagen for six months. He knew he would be paid a generous local allowance, and he could therefore save his London salary, not an insignificant sum of money, which one day might come very useful. He knew deep down he was probably also chosen as he was single, and therefore more likely to be focused on the job in hand without having to think or worry about family left behind at home.

*****

James had never set foot in Denmark before. He had heard so much about Copenhagen and was now looking forward to his stay. He felt he needed the change of scenery and the break from the monotonous life routine he was leading in London. During the week leading up to his departure, he sorted out what he needed to take with him. He tidied up his small house in St John's Wood. He checked his passport to ensure validity for the period and beyond. He put his financial affairs in order to ensure continuity of settling all his bills. He informed his neighbour on his right of his upcoming work plans as he needed someone to keep an eye on the property, and he knew he could trust Steve and Natalie. He organised his briefcase in which he would carry his laptop, his iPod and his kindle. As for his Golf, he drove it to his brother's house in Hereford to be kept there and used until he returns from Copenhagen. Finally the day for his departure arrived, a Saturday, and he set off to Gatwick airport in a taxi, arranged through his firm. He wandered round the free-shop area in the north terminal, bought himself CK1 eau de toilette, and sat down for a cup of coffee and a panini. His plane took off at 1 pm, and he enjoyed the ninety-minute flight in club class. At his destination he was impressed by Kastrup airport, and in no time at all was through all checks and out at arrivals where he was met by Hans who introduced himself as his colleague in Copenhagen's Borsen.

He liked Hans and felt warming up to him. Hans was tall, blue-eyed, with sharp features and blondish hair, who impressed

James with his excellent communication skills. Not only did he put James at ease from the outset but in few succinct sentences he managed to acquaint him with work, with his city bearings, and with what he needed to do to settle in nicely in his first week in Copenhagen. He drove him to his abode, a beautifully furnished two-bedroom apartment in Store Kongensgade, a broad street in the affluent part of the city, a few minutes walk from the Marmorkirke, the Marble Church. James liked his new but temporary home, which promised all comfort and an enjoyable stay in this charming capital. Along their way from the airport to his residence, James could glimpse that charm, and the reassurance that life would be exciting and attractive, and he could only hope that it would be matched by equally exciting and friendly work environment.

That evening James relaxed in his apartment. He liked his residence very much in the three-story apartment block. His was on the second floor with renaissance style windows. It had two bedrooms, each with an en-suite bathroom, a large lounge that has been divided into a sitting room proper and a dining area, the latter leading to a good sized kitchen through an archway which was fully equipped. The apartment looked and felt spacious, and James enjoyed the space all on one level. Thinking of his house back in London, he concluded that its surface area was equal but as it was divided over the two floors it made his English home feel smaller by comparison to his new Danish temporary abode. He glanced out of the window, and admired the elegant broad street called Store Konkensgade. He could see across the road diagonally from his place the elegant Phoenix Hotel. He settled into the comfortable sofa and set about discovering the various TV channels by flicking forward one program at a time. He was happy to see the BBC World channel for he wanted to keep in touch with what is happening back home and around the world. Later he prepared himself a hot snack of some Danish savoury that he found in the freezer compartment of the fridge, a dish of meat balls and pasta. It gave him a feeling of confidence about his new employer to think that they made the effort to ensure his comfort over the next few days, allowing him to settle in first without the need to rush to buy provisions in a new city where he would not know where to look to begin with for whatever he needed.

*****

James slept well overnight, the sleep of someone without worries or lingering thoughts. He woke up at eight, a lazy morning for him for a change, for he knew he would have to get up much earlier than that to be by 8.30 at the Borsen. He sipped his coffee sitting in the sofa, feeling relaxed and content, and later, once shaven, showered and dressed, he felt hungry enough to try the packet of organic muesli over some organic milk. It struck him how most of the food packets left for him had organic written all over the packaging. Maybe the dwellers of Copenhagen are health conscious, he thought.

By midday he was ready to explore. He made sure to put a light blazer on as it was still cool enough in Copenhagen at this time of year, and he set off. He thought of walking south first to investigate the route he would have to walk every morning to his work. The shops were shut, there were people already on the streets, and some were sitting for a bite or a drink in the open air, animated in their conversation with their companions who were also enjoying the restful Sunday outdoors. His steps took him to the King's New Square, dominated in the centre by the statue of King Christian V, himself on horse back with four classical figures submissively under his horse, and surrounded by impressive stately buildings, among them the French Embassy and the Hotel d'Angleterre. At the top right hand corner he could glimpse Nyhaven with its long canal and tall boats, and where throngs of people loitered or sat down at restaurants tables for their breakfast. He paused to admire the enormous square and its architecture before walking further south along the pedestrianised Stroget, with its abundance of shops, bars, restaurants and cafes. He found himself at the Caritas Fountain, and suddenly he could glimpse in the distance his place of work. He walked along the small canal, past the statue of Bishop Absalon, crossed the square, and stood face to face with the Borsen, giving his back to the water. And what a magnificent structure James thought. He felt proud to be working over the next six months in this magnificent looking long building with its green copper roof topped by a spire composed of four entwined dragon tails. He was content so far, and the whole enterprise of being and working in Copenhagen gave him a positive and promising impression.

He turned northwards and headed for the esplanade, as advised by Hans. As he strolled towards the Royal Palace he realised he was walking parallel to Kongensgade where he lived. The sun was shining and spreading its warmth, the breeze was gentle, and as he promenaded along the large sea estuary, James was already riding the silver lining. He felt relaxed and at ease with himself. He felt the excitement building up within him at the prospect of living and working in Copenhagen for the next six months, savouring new sceneries and experiencing new adventures and new people. He went past David's statue to his left, a replica of Michelangelo's, and he enjoyed the expanse of water to his right. Then he caught sight of Gefion fountain he had heard so much about, and as he approached, the whole spectacle unfolded before him. And he remembered the legend of the Nordic goddess Gefion who turned her four sons into oxen and used them to pull the island of Zealand from Sweden. He stood for a while in admiration of this fine enormous sculpture, and he gazed at the waterfall cascading down. He paid a little visit to the beautiful Anglican church behind the fountain before walking on, still along the water edge through delightful gardens.

All of a sudden there she was, in the distance, appearing smaller than he had thought, with throngs of people buzzing around her and at her feet, many jumping over the stones surrounding the base just to get closer or to touch her. There she was, Den Lille Havfrue, as she is known in Danish, The Little Mermaid. James felt a different emotion from what he had been experiencing so far since he arrived. He was not sure why this was, but as he got closer and closer, almost level with the statue, he felt a strong attraction and his entire being was somewhat overwhelmed and agitated. He remembered Andersen's fairytale of this tragic sea-girl who exchanged her voice for human legs in order to gain the love of an earthly prince, but had to watch in silence as he jilted her for a human princess. And he remembered how in desperation she had thrown herself into the sea again and had turned into foam.

James stood looking at the mermaid statue from the higher ground, and could only disagree strongly with what people had recounted to him. How could they say she was unassuming, he thought. James stared at the girl sitting on the large rock, the head turned to her right, looking sad and pensive. He perceived a cute pretty face, and a shapely beautiful body, with well formed breasts and rounded and proportionate thighs culminating into the large fin tucked underneath her. James thought her little bulge of a tummy increased her beauty and sex appeal, and he saw how wonderful her pose was, supporting herself on her right hand against the rock. James fell instantly in love, and wished he could also get a glimpse of her back which was towards the sea. He loved her delicate face, her short hair, and the sense of femininity and finesse she radiated to the onlooker. James pushed his way through the crowd and climbed down onto the step stones to get closer to this enchanting girl. He risked getting his shoes and even his socks wet just to touch this girl's hand. And he did, while glancing at her attractive and charming face and torso, feeling enchanted to his core as he did so. Once back up on the esplanade he was lucky to find an empty bench right opposite this silent girl he now considered his beloved.

The little mermaid was James's ideal girl, the one he had dreamt all his adult life about, the girl he was hoping he would meet one day, his twin soul. This mermaid of a girl was the personification of the feminine, sensitive, intelligent girl he always hoped she would share his life, the one who would understand him and come to occupy his heart and his mind. He had not met her yet, but there she was, though inanimate, yet to him full of life and charm, calling to him by his name, telling him I am the one you have been searching for, for I have been existing for you, so that our like souls should love one other. Time flew as James sat gazing at the mermaid, the sun was setting behind him, and the air grew cooler and biting. He put his blazer on which he had taken off earlier, and all within him he felt emotionally agitated and his heart fluttering. Why would this half woman half mermaid have not been fully human like him, meeting her right here at this very spot, both of them finding each other and falling in love, a normal encounter like so many all over the world, and a normal finale like so many who fall in love, thought James. He gazed at his girl, for he saw her only as his ideal girl, and said goodbye with a lasting look, telling her he would be back everyday, for he has fallen in love. He made his way back to his abode, day dreamed as he sat on the sofa, and took himself eventually to bed, all moved and overwhelmed.

*****

James woke up next morning geared up for his first day at his new working place. He took extra care that morning to look his best, knowing that the first impression is always the best and the lasting. Blue was always his colour in such circumstances, which somehow projected his handsome face and figure. He matched the plain Daniel Hechter blue shirt with a blue striped tie that he had bought in Sorrento the previous year while holidaying. He walked south towards the Caritas Fountain through King's New Square, and made his way to the left, along the canal, to the Borsen, retracing his footsteps of the day before. He reached the Borsen, climbed the few granite steps leading to the entrance, and stepped inside to be met by the guard. The formalities of issuing him with an ID photofit card and a badge were concluded promptly, and he was led along what looked like a medieval corridor to a large hall which, James thought, must have served as a banqueting hall in times gone by. Off the hall, he was ushered into a large office where he was introduced to Ditter Grand, the Borsen Director. Ditter welcomed James with open arms and exclaimed

' Welcome James. I have received high recommendations about you from London, and Hans has not stopped praising you. Welcome to the Borsen. I hope you will find working here pleasant and interesting. I also hope you already have settled well in your apartment, and that you find Copenhagen to your liking. '

James thanked Mr Grand for his kind words and assured him that he has been well looked after from the moment he landed in Copenhagen. He added ' I am really looking forward to working in this magnificent building, and enrich myself with not just what this charming city has to offer but also with what I shall learn working here. '

' I am confident you will. '

Mr Grand picked up the phone, went through the menu button, and was heard saying ' Hans, please come over. James is in my office. '

A few moments later Hans came in, and he was entrusted by the Borsen Director with James.

Hans took James to their office, a medium-sized room, comfortably furnished, on the ground floor, from where James could see through the window the water canal he had passed earlier on. He admired the view and commented on it to Hans. The first day at work was a general introduction in how the Borsen runs, and James was later introduced to the colleagues working in the other offices and with whom he would have to deal. During the lunch break, Hans took him to the Borsen canteen on the upper floor, and over the meal they chatted away. The time passed quickly, and suddenly it was five o'clock, and time to leave. James walked back to his apartment, but as he approached his abode, he felt the urge to see the Mermaid. He knew he had to see her everyday. He went past his apartment, and soon was standing on the elevated ground gazing at her.

James's mind was racing. He was aware of an emotion that was running through his body and stirring him to the core. He tried to comprehend, to search for an answer, to fathom how could someone simply fall in love with an inanimate woman. Did he say fall in love? He realised that that is what he thought and felt, but then how, he kept asking himself. It is true that this statue of a mermaid has come to resemble exactly the woman he wanted to fall in love with. Why would she not have been a real person, in flesh and blood, his misery would have been at an end. He sat down on the same bench he sat in the day before. He was now fixing the Mermaid with his eyes, and he could not take his eyes off her. And he felt his heart fluttering, his being seized by an overwhelming desire to go to her, hold her hand, caress her face, and embrace her with all his strength. If he were to do just that, people would think he was mad or probably jesting or making fun. And yet he realised it was the truth, he was in love with the Mermaid, Andersen's

Mermaid, and that there was no escape. He was ready to love with all his might, with all his heart, with all his soul, but providence had not been kind to him yet, unhelpful, unyielding, when it could have created the chance of meeting a girl just like the Mermaid. He felt sad, disheartened, that it had not happened, and scared at the same time that it may never happen. So for now, he would be in love with the Mermaid, and he would dream, he would talk to her, think about her, long to see her and be with her, and she would be only his in his heart, and he would not mind the thousands of admirers who flock to see her every day.

It was time to go home, and he said goodbye to his Mermaid, but not before going down and balancing on the few stones in the water to caress her hand. He believed she knew what was in his heart, that he loved her, and he thought from the way she looked at him when their gaze met, that she was aware of his presence. Once in his apartment, he settled to his usual routine, preparing himself a meal, catching up on the news on BBC World, checking his e-mail on his iPad, and falling asleep once in bed having wired himself to his iPod to listen to Beethoven's Moonlight sonata.

The days followed each other, he had been working at the Borsen a month, and the London office were satisfied with the outcome of the amber gem commodities he was working on.

Everyday, James went to see the Mermaid. His love had not abated, and all he wanted was to be with her, look at her, touch her, and talk to her in his mind. He felt her sadness, her loneliness, her sensitive soul, and many a time he felt like crying out ' Come to me beloved, get up and walk across, shed that curse that is enchaining you, for I am here, I have been looking for you all my life, and you have been waiting for me, and it is meant that we should be reunited. How could I go on without you, and why would you stay tied down to this stone, melancholic, unable to share in the most beautiful of emotions, to love and be loved. I have long searched for you, and now that I have found you, you have been silent, fated to be silent for eternity, and you and I are destined to suffer for eternity.

*****

James came to be with the Mermaid every evening after work - it was spring moving onto summer - and every weekend when he spent even longer hours. He felt he needed to be there, but he was not one to fantasise or daydream. For the moment the Mermaid was his girl and his beloved. He could indulge in loving her, touching her, talking to her, and hoping for the future, when one day she may materialise in flesh, the very girl who strolled through his mind.

Several weeks after arriving in Copenhagen, James made his way one Saturday as usual to sit in the bench facing the Mermaid. The sun was glorious, spring had finally arrived in earnest, the trees were blossoming, and the skies were a mixture of serene blue and golden rays. On that day the crowds were thronging to see his Mermaid, and there was much jostling for places and great fun abounding around him. Though at times he felt irritated when people blocked the view to his beloved, he nevertheless was proud that people found her so attractive and so imposing. On that day he noticed a small wooden hut on wheels, serving hot and cold drinks, and manned by what looked like a young girl, who had her back to him. The trolley was engulfed by people, all after a drink of some sort, some asking for a bottle of water or a can of fizzy drink, and others, the more mature in age, seeking tea or coffee, served in a plastic mug. He could see a large kettle with a lead attached to a large battery, and various pots containing a variety of seeds and tea bags. James felt the need to clear his head, and he decided to get himself a cup of coffee. He joined the lumpy queue, and when his turn came he asked for coffee with milk. As he looked up at the girl to hand her the twenty krona as marked at the top of the wooden enclosure, he gasped. Looking at him with a gentle smile and a radiant face all he could see was the Mermaid, and as he gasped his lips said in a faltering whisper 'the Mermaid'. He looked behind him towards the statue sitting on the stone, in an involuntary jerk, his whole being shaken, but there she was, still sitting in her assumed position, still pensive and melancholic, his beloved, who had not stirred an inch. James once again looked at the girl, trying to regain his composure while at the same time struggling to understand. The girl said to him

' I look like her. Everyone says so. It is just a coincidence. I have seen many people reacting, but I have never seen the reaction I have seen on your face. You looked shocked. '

' Pardon me, I must have been engrossed in the Mermaid earlier on, that when I saw your face I must have felt I was seeing a vision. I am sure it is what we call deja-vu. Please accept my apologies. '

While James was recovering from his ordeal, the girl had already prepared him his coffee drink. But James was still mesmerised, he knew it was her, after so many years of longing, the one who would occupy his heart alone, the source of its happiness, and it would be the end of his quest, and the dream becoming a reality. He was not going to let go, for this was her, now in flesh, talking to him, gazing at him with a tilt of the head, the angelic face, the soft attractive eyes, and the bursting femininity, exactly how he had imagined her to be, and surely how he wanted her to be.

James felt the compulsion to hold onto her. He hesitated before saying

' Do you come here everyday? If you do not mind, perhaps I can escort you later when you pack up your amazing vehicle. I am James. '

People were continuing to queue, and so the girl motioned him to step aside and said

' OK, I pack up in one hour. I shall wait for you. I am Christiana. '

James retreated to go and sit on the bench but the space had been taken by an elderly woman. He did not want to be far from Christiana, and so he sat on a low wall stretching behind the bench to both sides. He could not control his emotions, and could not divert his gaze away from the girl. Christiana carried on in her tasks, but from time to time she glanced furtively towards James. She was able to concentrate on what she was doing, but there was a new emotion taking hold of her, something she knew was totally different, something beautiful and reassuring, an emotion of contentment and submission.

An hour later, James suddenly woke up from his reverie, when he saw Christiana packing up her trolley. It all folded up and in neatly, and was now resembling a large pram. He stood up and took a few steps forward. Christiana pushed the trolley towards James, and once level with him she stopped, and looked at him with an expression on her face that said 'What am I going to do with you?'. It was James who spoke first but all he could utter was 'Christiana'!
Christiana lowered her eyes and said
' I walk this way to go home. '

James walked side by side with her but was still unable to say anything else. He knew he was in love, deeply in love, and if he felt terrified, it was not because of the situation but because of the fear that he would lose her, and that the relationship was only going to last as long as this encounter lasted.

Christiana said ' I know you are not Danish '.
James managed to untie his tongue and said ' I am English, I am in Copenhagen for six months, working at the Borsen. I am here for just over four months more before I return to England. I have a home in London '.

Christiana looked at James and was about to say something but stopped. James could see that. Then suddenly she said ' What do you …' but did not continue. Her voice betrayed an emotional struggle, for she found in James the man of her dreams, physically and intellectually, and wondered as she walked side by side with him, whether this was fated. She could tell, not just from his attire and his movements that he was genuine, but also from his face and his struggle to control his emotions that these were also genuine and truthful.

' So you are in finance or investment banking ! What a coincidence, I am a final year student at the University of Copenhagen, studying accountancy and finance. The university is very old dating back to 1476. One of its graduates was Soren Kierkegaard. My campus is on the outskirts of the city, but I come often to the main buildings in the city centre. As I am specialising in international accountancy, some of the classes are in English and German, but usually in Danish. '

Christiana suddenly blurted all that out and waited for James's response. Poor man, she thought to herself, he looks totally overwhelmed. So she continued, feeling a compulsion to tell him everything about herself.
' I live with my mother, not far from here. My father died when I was ten years old. '

James mustered all his courage, he felt it was time to do so, and said,
' I like you Christiana, I liked you the moment I saw you, and I want us to see each other again.

'He hesitated before continuing ' It's like I have finally found you '.

Christiana stopped and looked at James. Her eyes shone with slight moisture, and reflected her happiness and her relief that the few minutes they were spending together were not the beginning and the end, and yet at the same time they were imploring for the future, that she was not ready for a sad ending, for an end to a dream only now conceived but which had been dormant in her heart and her mind for a number of years.

They had been walking for twenty minutes, when Christiana said
' My home is along the side street just coming. '
' Will you be doing the same tomorrow? ' asked James.
' No, tomorrow is Sunday. I spend some time with my mother, catching up on the week gone and on the house chores, as I get home late and I spend the evenings with my head in the books '.
Christiana smiled and said ' I can be free from midday '.
' I shall be waiting at this corner tomorrow at twelve '.
' OK then '.

Christiana wanted to touch James, this young man of her dreams, who had appeared from nowhere but who was already taking possession of her heart. She put her right hand forward and James slipped his in hers. The hands encounter lasted several seconds, not as a greeting sign, but as the acknowledgement that they were united, that they belonged to each other, and that their feelings were mutual and reciprocated.

*****

James could not sleep overnight. He kept thinking of Christiana. Has providence finally had pity on him, he asked himself. He went over all that happened the afternoon of the day before. It had all been real, very real, as if the Mermaid had had life breathed into her. He had met Christiana, the embodiment of his dream girl, who somehow was the mirror image of the Mermaid, and now his hard quest was over, and she was with him, and he could count on it. With eyes closed, he pictured Christiana a thousand times, and she was definitely his dream girl, the long chestnut hair which she had put in a bun, the soft attractive pale blue eyes, the angelic face, the delicate skin, the dainty hands, and above all the intelligent mind and the beautiful smile. And he was not letting go, he would pledge love to eternity, and he would cherish her and keep her safe. He could not wait for dawn to make its debut, and it would only be six more hours to seeing his beloved.

Christiana could not sleep either. She could not even devote much time to her mother that evening, so consumed were her mind and her heart with this new emotion she had not experienced before. She thought about James, and asked herself what made her accept that he should accompany her on her way home. She was not one to indulge in such fantasies, but it was not reason that was now governing her behaviour, but her heart. Could it be love at first sight, she asked herself, something she had never envisaged before. She certainly liked James, the way he looked and the way he talked and moved, and as she lay down in bed she was even more aware of those flutters that were emanating from her heart, and which she had lost all control over. She felt concerned lest she was moving to a troubled time at a time when she needed all her energy to finish her degree, for the final exams were only three months away. She finally fell asleep, approaching dawn, from sheer tiredness. When she woke up it was mid morning, something she had not done for a very long time, and which worried her mother.

Christiana maintained the normal Sunday morning routine, and then informed her mother that she needed to meet a friend in the city, something to do with her university studies. She took special care in her appearance that day, and decided to wear a pink dress which had some attractive decorative buttons, and she let her long chestnut hair down. At midday she left the tiny house and walked down the street towards the corner junction, physically aware of her thumping heartbeat, not knowing what to expect. But there he was, in a blending blue outfit, holding a pink rose, and as she approached James, her lips trembled and her legs felt weak, and wondered how could he have guessed that she was going to wear pink, that he brought her a matching rose. James stood rooted to the spot, admiring this girl that he was now loving passionately, the radiant face, the gleaming eyes, and the slender figure. And as Christiana got closer she felt the urge to embrace her man who had taken possession of her heart, and she found herself putting her arms round his neck and resting her head on his left shoulder. They both knew then that it had happened, that cupid had pierced them with the arrow of love, and that they were united body and soul in an eternal love and in their desire to keep each other's company for as long as they live, loving each other through their youth and into their mature years. A little pearl rolled down Christiana's left cheek. They walked silently, side by side, Christiana holding onto James's right arm, and they felt enveloped in a cloud of happiness, oblivious of the world around them, enjoying the serenity and the passion which were radiating from each one of them to the other.

They reached the Royal Danish Playhouse and James suggested they sat down in its open air cafe, overlooking the large sea estuary.

After ordering two coffees, James said
' I could not sleep last night, having found you, the one and only treasure I have been looking for, I was apprehensive should I

lose you the moment I found you, and I am not letting go Christiana. '
' How do you know you have found the right person ? ' came her reply.
' I just know '.

They did not need to say much more, whatever they felt for each other was being conveyed in their gaze and their voice, and they wondered each in their own mind why they had not met or known each other long before. They talked about their circumstances, James's parents dying when he was younger as they had married when older, and his bond with his older brother who is married with two very young children. He told her about London which Christiana had not travelled to, and about his job. In her turn, Christiana talked about her wonderful mother, and the few memories she remembers of her father, and about her hopes for the future in her chosen career. Time flew, they walked back the way they came, always along the water edge, and they felt their love for each other strengthening. By the time they reached Christiana's little house, they had agreed to see each other everyday if possible, but also agreed that Christiana's studies should be given ample time and priority even if it meant not seeing each other on some days. The sun had set, they realised they had been together for several hours. And when the time came to say good bye, they felt attracted to each other in a gripping emotion, and their lips met in a long kiss, and their arms in a long embrace, and they experienced extreme happiness, a happiness that comes from heart turmoil.

*****

Over the following weeks, James and Christiana made it a habit to meet everyday, even if it meant stealing just brief moments.

At weekends, they had more time to enjoy each other, and as the days passed they grew very attached to one another, and the love bond was such that they could read each other's mind without the need to express their thoughts in words. Christiana took James one day to the change of guards at the Royal Palace, and on another day they visited together Christianborg Palace where James admired the beautiful and ornate library. James understood Christiana's need for adequate time to attend to her studies, for the end of year exams were drawing near, and they were both hopeful and confident of a graduation with top marks. They had discussed the possibility that Christiana would move to London, where James hoped he could vouch for her with his employer and probably secure for her a placement for six months or longer to begin with. They had mapped their future, Christiana would move in with him, get herself on the career ladder, and they would eventually get married.

Christiana brought James home to meet her mother. She had to break the news of her love at some stage, and her mother was not surprised to hear it, as she had noticed the change on her daughter, and had wondered so many times if her daughter was not in love, but she refrained from asking the question, knowing that she would get to know about it all in good time. Christiana's mother accepted whole-heartedly her daughter's plan to move to London, and hoped that she would find happiness with James, whom she liked, feeling intuitively as a mother that it would be so.

A week before James was due to return to London, Christiana obtained her university degree with honours, and James took her to Kong Hans Kaelder to celebrate, a lovely cellar restaurant with swooping gothic arches, one of Denmark's finest which serves classical French cuisine. They toasted champagne to Christiana's success, to their love story, and to their future happiness.

James's colleagues at the Borsen threw a lunch party on the occasion of his departure, and he was presented with a parting gift of fine porcelain from the famous Royal Copenhagen Porcelain store. On the eve of his departure, James dined with Christiana and her mother at their home, and they feasted on Gravad Laks, the Scandinavian delicacy of salmon served with a creamy sauce of oil, mustard and sugar, followed by a main course of small cuts of tenderloin pork with boiled potatoes, onions and gravy, all prepared by Christiana's mother. Christiana's eyes seemed to say to James 'I love you', which, typical of the fine lady that she was, she had not yet uttered once. James understood this very well, it did not have to be spoken, but which was implied and visible in her gestures, her caring, and in her outward emotions. He had on his part declared his love for Christiana in those three simple words, that have existed since the dawn of time.

Christiana accompanied James to Kastrup Airport the next day for his flight, and at the departure gate she held onto him convulsively. She was crying. James pressed her tightly to him, and his right hand was caressing her long hair. Both remained silent, and it was James who eventually spoke
' It is only a matter of a few weeks, and it will be my turn to wait for you at Heathrow. I have already emailed my boss at the firm, and he seems to think he can arrange a placement for you. I would never have thought I had to come to Denmark to find the woman I have always loved before I met. '
They embraced, and James planted a long kiss on Christiana's lips. Then he produced from his pocket a small jewellery case. Christiana opened it to find a golden ring with a small solitary amber gem mounted on it.
' I love you ' James said.
' I love you ' said Christiana.
It was time for James to go in, and Christiana stood motionless, her hands across her chest, watching James disappear through

the crowd heading for security check, until she could see him no more.

Back in London, James had to present a detailed report of his activities at the Borsen in Copenhagen, and he was congratulated on a job well done, which has benefited Solomon & Solomon, extending their business to the amber market. James was delighted to hear that Christiana could start working in the firm in a couple of months, and he was even more delighted to hear that she would be paid a modest salary. Christiana was ecstatic to hear this bit of news, and she was all geared up for her forthcoming move to London, doing all the necessary preparations. She and James were on the phone to each other daily, longing for when they would be together.

The time for Christiana's arrival to London was getting closer, and it was now only two weeks away. That day, Christiana did not answer her mobile phone when James called. When he tried later in the day, again unsuccessfully, he began to worry. He rang Christiana's home but neither Christiana nor her mother picked up the phone. He decided to text and to email, and having sent several of either to no avail, he was beginning to despair, not knowing what could have happened. He was up all night pacing his house, worrying that calamity must have happened to either Christiana or her mother, and the thought that it could have happened to Christiana made him the more miserable. He dismissed any other possibility as the reason, he had already crossed that threshold of not finding favour with her, for he had found her, the love was reciprocated, and she was his. He tossed in his mind the endless possibilities of illness or accident. He absented from work the next day, feeling agitated and at the same time down and very worried. He tried several times to reach either Christiana or her home. Around midday his mobile phone rang. The number that registered was Christiana's home. James's heart missed a beat. At the other end was Christiana's mother, and she was tearful. She said

' I am sorry James I could not answer your calls yesterday. " Christiana's mother hesitated, clearly in distress, before resuming
' Christiana has been admitted to hospital. They think she has myocarditis. '
' And how is she? ' asked James.
' She is very unwell at present. She has been asking about you. ' was the reply.
' Don't worry Mother, Christiana will make it. I am coming today. Which hospital is she in? '
' They have taken her to the highly specialised Rigshospitalet ' replied the mother.
James promised to be with them the very day.

James's world fell apart. His beloved, his Mermaid was gravely ill. He had found her, and Providence, which had initially helped him, was now working against him. No, it was not fair, he concluded. Providence cannot in the same token offer happiness and then claim it back. Christiana will not have it, will not accept this poor deal, and together they would fight it.

James, in a flash, prepared a small hand luggage with all necessary items, and headed for the airport in a taxi. On the way he checked the internet for flights to Copenhagen that very day. He did not find any seats on direct flights, and managed to secure an indirect flight via Oslo on Norwegian Airlines. When he finally landed in Kastrup Airport, it was evening. He hailed a taxi to the hospital, and contacted Christiana's mother before getting there, who was now carrying her daughter's mobile. She came down to the hospital entrance to escort him to the intensive care. Her eyes were red and bloodshot from crying. As they made their way in, she prepared him for the fact that Christiana had been very ill for forty-eight hours, and that the virus had got hold of her heart, which is showing signs of failing. James burst out crying. He did not know what to say or what to do. When they entered the room where Christiana was being nursed, and seeing all the drips, the oxygen mask, and all the monitors, he felt a desperate man, drained from all hope, clutching to a miracle, seeing his life ebbing away, and suffering at Christiana's suffering, suffering at the realisation that the happiness they had both dreamt of might not be realised after all. As he glanced at the ECG monitor, he could see the trace expanding into various shapes of troughs and arcs, and he knew in his mind that this was a bad sign, for he had seen traces before, on the big screen and the small screen, but what he was witnessing now was a failing heart, a heart that was going out of control, and heading for an exit.

As he stood next to the bed, distraught, losing his mind, Christiana opened her eyes and looked first at her mother and then at James, her eyes telling them both that she loves them and that she will always love them. She tried to move her right hand but could not, and James reached for it, and put his hand in hers, and they both remembered the first time they had done the same, when she was serving cold and hot drinks and he had come looking for his Mermaid. Christiana found it tiring and closed her eyes, and she knew this was her last view on the world, and her last breath, and that she had closed her eyes for the last time. She died surrounded by the two people she lived to love. Her generous and loving heart had stopped beating. Her mother slumped over her and covered her with kisses. James fell down on his knees, and kissed Christiana's hand, as he had done before, but this time for the last time.

*****

James decided to stay in Copenhagen until after the funeral. The next day he made his way to the mermaid. It was still early morning. He sat on the bench, and gazed at the statue. He could not stop his tears. He had met his Mermaid and she had been taken from him. He had loved her and she had loved him, and he was now left with his memories, and his love for her which will never extinguish. He gazed at that other mermaid, the inanimate, sad and pensive one, and wondered whether she was aware of the pain he was going through. This mermaid was the incarnate image of his Mermaid, and he would be back time and time again, in all the years left to his life, sitting there and remembering the woman he had fallen in love with so passionately, and who inhabits his heart for eternity, never forgetting her and never ceasing to love her.

****

MY ENCOUNTER WITH A SHARK

I went for a deep swim at the beach Platja Nova Icaria in Barcelona, about 150 metres from the shore. The sea was calm, I was just floating, relaxed and not making much effort, and enjoying the view of the seashore. Suddenly a big grey thing popped out of the water about ten metres from me, and started coming towards me, with a menacing and aggressive attitude. When it came face to face with me, our noses almost touching, I realised it was a shark. I shouted at it " What's your problem ? Just calm down will you ". The shark seemed to be taken aback then said " You are not trying to counsel me are you ? ". I said " Listen, I am harmless ". It appeared to give it a thought and then suddenly it calmed down and opened up its heart, as if it wanted to talk and get it off its chest. It said " I never knew my parents, I suffered domestic violence, I have an arthritic fin. " I suggested to it that it becomes vegetarian, and starts to feed on planktons. We talked for a while, and then it said it needed to get back to its two youngsters as it is a single parent. We both promised to meet again the next day at the same time and same spot.

*****

Requinette appeared at the appointed time and place for our rendez-vous. It is a she shark, and that's her name, she told me. She brought along her two little ones who would not float still and who kept swimming round and round. Requinette and I swam from Platja de Nova Icaria to the next beach Platja Bogatel, and back again, with the little ones tagging along. Requinette told me that she was originally from the ocean. Her ex-partner left her one day and swam away. She later heard he is leading a life of crime and is known as the Great White. She thinks it is only a matter of time before he is caught and fed on platters to diners in Seaport, New York.

Requinette found it extremely difficult to survive on her own with her two babies, as food was scarce and she ran the risk of shark bait, Or-Ka ! She took her young family and relocated to the Mediterranean. She found it pleasant but the sea water too warm. Again it was not easy to make ends meet but at least there was no shark bait, Or-Ka. Requinette kept repeating this Or-Ka so many times that I said " Hey, I think you have OCD ". Anyway, Requinette found the coral where she settled hostile and unwelcoming, for they do not like strangers. Life became too stressful and she got hooked on eating sardines which was not good for her health. The young ones, feeling alienated and unable to join in with the kids activities began to display antisocial behaviour.

It was time to return ashore, as the life guard was by now whistling frantically and looked extremely nervous. I said good bye to this new fishy acquaintance, and we arranged to meet again the following day.

As I swam back it suddenly dawned on me that everyone was out of the sea, with the crowd standing at the edge of the water, all watching my encounter with Requinette. As I got out there was a thunder of applause, and suddenly I found the media taking photos and fighting to interview me. I had now become a celebrity overnight out of notoriety.

*****

I saw Requinette for the last time today. She brought along her two little ones, Requino and Requina. We swam from Platja de Nova Icaria to Platja Bogatel and on to Platja Marbella, and back. She seemed to be happy, and had a beaming grin, which can look worrying. She told me that yesterday on their way back they stumbled on a small rock island inhabited by only a mermaid whose name is Calypso. I exclaimed " Oh no, not Calypso who imprisoned Odysseus for ten years. " She said " "

" That's the one, and I think she is misunderstood. She was married to a whale tycoon, but went for unreasonable behaviour and left him. The rock island was her good settlement. Requino and Requina took to Calypso straight away, and she seemed to have both the motherly and the fatherly devotion. She has been lonely ever since she felt pity for Odysseus and let him return home to his Penelope, and on my part I had to think of my little ones future and of my needs, and we decided to settle with Calypso and become one family, and parents to the kids. I have no desire to work in the sea, and Calypso is quite happy to provide. " I noticed some cuts on the little ones, and Requinette told me that it was their way of releasing their frustration by cutting themselves against the rocks.

It was time to say farewell, and we embraced, but I felt their rough skin, which if you are not careful can hurt you. The family swam on to their new life, and I swam back to my world, the world that I know.

****

MAX

Max lives on the other side of the village. He occupies the upper floor of a property and runs a shop on the ground floor. There is depth to the property which extends a distance to the back. The shop is therefore large and it sells outdated stationary and useless paperback stories. At least that is what I think. Something else I also think is that the employees in that shop are miserable and pursued unjustly by Max. The impression you get when you step into that shop is that it is an institution for offenders. Everyone is seen by Max as an offender, and he keeps coming up with more and more sinister ways of supervising them. He punishes even if there is no mistake committed, and he threatens even though he knows he cannot survive without his subordinates or find replacement for them. And all around him he only sees offenders who need to be shown what he believes is his visionary way, which by the way changes from day to day depending on his whims. Poor souls I tell myself, they have really come unstuck, for you see, working for Max is considered a setback in their career if they wanted to look for another placement. And on their faces, all you see, is stress and despair, and moreover, they all need anger management. And if a customer browsing in the shop happens to frown unintentionally, for Max it becomes a sign of dissatisfaction which means loss of profit, and poor soul of employee who happens to be serving that customer at the time. According to Max's rule of thumb, it must be the employee's fault, for after all they are offenders by definition and therefore by habit.

To tell you the truth, I have had enough of Max and his antics and I have decided never to go near his shop again. And there is nothing I can do for his offenders. They will all remain there until they either drop dead or end up dispatched to see a Shrink !

IN SEARCH OF LOVE

(A Sequel to James and the Little Mermaid)

James sat on the same bench he had sat in before, time and time again, gazing at the Mermaid. He was in Copenhagen, and had come on one of his regular visits to this city. Every three months he flew there to spend a weekend, not to sightsee but to sit and gaze at the Mermaid, and to remember. His soul was sad and agitated, and it had not found the inner peace ever since he lost Christiana a year before. And whenever he was at this spot, his eyes would get moist and all he could think of was his departed beloved. And time and time again, he would stare at the Mermaid, his Mermaid, and beg of her to answer the question that had been eating him for the past twelve months. On this particular occasion, his soul was enveloped in much greater sadness, for the next day it would be the first anniversary of losing Christiana. And he felt like screaming at the Mermaid, that providence had been cruel to him, and that she, the Mermaid, had witnessed it all and had remained silent and neutral. She had not taken his side, she had allowed it all to happen, and had watched in silence the heartbreak and the decimation of his happiness. The images were now floating on the water surface around the Mermaid. He saw Christiana when he first set eyes on her, he saw her walking side by side with him, and he saw her putting her arms round his neck in her pink dress. The images kept coming, the happy times they spent in and around Copenhagen, their embraces and their intimate love, and the day she passed her final year exams when they went out celebrating. He remembered his declaration of love in the weeks before, and their farewell at Kastrup airport. And finally he remembered her lying ill in bed at the hospital, and closing her eyes on him for the last time.

James was feeling the pain, his heart was aching, his soul was so distraught, that he finally broke down and shed some tears. He had cried at Christiana's funeral, and had felt the sadness day in day out ever since. But today his sadness was all consuming, he had lost the one girl he had all his life been searching for, and when he found her it had to end. Christiana's mother had not been able to take in the tragic death of her only daughter and had died of a heart attack a few months later. She had been his solace during his previous visits but she had also gone, and he thought she must be reunited with her beautiful loving daughter.

James knew deep down that he had not recovered from the loss of Christiana, and he realised that he may never do so. He had put all his heart desires in the girl of his dream, that having lost her the moment he found her was bound to hurt for the rest of his life. Sadness had taken hold of him, he was no longer able to enjoy life as others do, and as it should be for someone of his age. He felt that life was somehow punishing him, and he could not understand why. What was it that he had done that he deserved such misfortune, he always pondered, but he was going to continue to love Christiana with all his soul and all his strength even though she was no longer on earth to be on the receiving end of his unconditional love. James was aware of all this, and did not think he could forget or recover.

Once back in London two days later he felt he needed some more time off, perhaps a longer time, for he felt he needed to heal. He was aware that his grief at the loss of Christiana had not shifted and that his bereavement was not complete. His heart and his mind were in turmoil, and he needed direction and guidance. He turned up for work as usual at his investment bank, and coped as much as he could during the week, but he knew his mind was not totally on the job. He was constantly absorbed in his memories, the pain was still hard to endure, and the idea of a sabbatical leave of some weeks or even months began to take hold in his mind. He phoned his brother John in Hereford and asked him if he could come and stay the weekend with them. John was his older brother and married to Sophie, with two young children. James always turned to his brother for direction and for guidance whenever he was troubled by anything of a grave magnitude. So Friday after work, he packed up a small bag of a change of clothing and his toiletries, and headed for Hereford in his golf car. Two hours later he was being welcomed by John and Sophie. His two little nieces, Stephanie and Veronica jumped at his neck. James felt somehow relieved of his burden of sadness and grief, being surrounded by all the family love, and they all sat down to an appetising dinner cooked by Sophie. There was banter from the little girls, and much attention from Sophie, for which James was fully grateful and appreciative.

After the meal, Sophie took the children to the study to allow her husband and his brother to have their talk in private. Sophie was a sensitive person who always knew what to do when and in what proportion, and this sensitivity allowed her to gage situations and to respond in a timely and proportionate manner to people's emotional needs and upheavals.
James and John sat opposite each other at the dining table, and James's eyes were lowered as if he was inspecting with some gravity the large tablecloth with its embroidery. The fingers of his right hand were fiddling with bits of crumbs, his left elbow on the table with the hand supporting his chin. John broke the silence and said,

' So, how was Copenhagen? '

James sighed but did not respond. John sensed his brother discomfiture and continued,

' James, I know you are still feeling sad and I can see it, we can all see it, but it is a year now, and frankly, I do not think you should allow yourself to continue in this mood, it does not serve any purpose, it will not change events or bring back Christiana from the dead, and all it does is ruin your health and stop you from living your life. Life goes on, James, life can be cruel but it goes on for everyone, and we should allow misfortunes to happen, but it does not mean that everything stops indefinitely. You have good memories, happy memories, and that is how they should be, happy memories, not sad memories. '

John stopped to give his brother a breather before continuing

' You need to pick yourself up, you need to look life in the eye, and move on. You will find love again, but that is not for the time being. Sophie and I were discussing this yesterday and she suggested some time off, perhaps abroad, not in Denmark of course, but away from the scenery or the environment that is connected with the past, a time to reflect, to admire nature, to visit places and to meet people, and hopefully this will do you a world of good. Actually Sophie knows a family in Bavaria who own a Hoff in the village of Oberammergau. She believes the rooms are very comfortable with en-suite facilities, and the village offers panoramic views of the Bavarian Alps. I think you should take a break from work of a few weeks and go and spend some time in Bavaria, I am sure the beautiful nature will heal you in no time at all. Sophie can tell you about the place and her friend. '

' Sophie ' John called.
Sophie came in half guessing why she was needed at this precise moment.

' I have just been telling James about your friend and her family in Oberammergau. '

' Oh ', said Sophie, ' my friend Ursula, yes, they have a lovely Hoff and all rooms have magnificent views over the Alps. From there you can travel in whichever direction you wish and you will always come across either scenic spots or beautiful palaces. I spent a summer once there and it has been my best holiday ever, sorry Darling you have given me some wonderful holidays, but this place, Oh, something really special. I am sure

Ursula would be able to take you around or tell you where to go and what to visit. Their food is also gorgeous. I met Ursula on an exchange visit when I was at secondary school, and we have remained good friends ever since. She is yet to accept my invitation to come and spend some time with us. I can give her a ring and make all arrangements for you. I do hope you will decide to go. You will nor regret it. '

Sophie said all this with continuity that bordered on the rehearsal beforehand. James was thinking, while looking from John to Sophie and from Sophie to John. He was weighing everything in his mind, and suddenly he felt that somehow that was what he should be doing, to go away, to try and forget all, to let his soul and his mind escape the flow of the daily routine that was enchaining him, and to try to rediscover his self once again.

' Yes ', came the reply, ' I want to go. I shall ask for a three-month sabbatical leave. I am sure it will do me some good. I hope the rooms are not expensive, as I shall not be earning a salary during all that time. "

' I think the rooms are reasonably priced, and meals are included ', replied Sophie.

It was all then agreed, Sophie would contact her friend, a room would be arranged, and James thought the sooner the better, and therefore he would be ready to leave in a week's time. He spent the rest of the weekend with his brother and his family, feeling less uptight and at the same time grateful that his brother had, once again, come to the rescue, like he always did, and has put him on the right road to self recovery.

James worked the next week, saw his supervisor who reluctantly agreed for a three-month sabbatical leave, and by the end of the week he was ready to fly to Munich. He informed his neighbours Steve and Natalie to keep an eye on his property, and he packed a large suitcase with enough clothes to last a couple of weeks at a time. Finally the day arrived, and he headed to Heathrow airport for his ninety-minute flight to Munich airport.

****

Upon arrival in Munich Airport, James hired a car, an Opel model, and headed west towards Oberammergau. In an hour he was in this village, and as he drove through the narrow streets he admired the local houses, each with painting adorning their facade, all representing various scenes from the life of Jesus. He already knew, having researched beforehand, that Oberammergau is the setting for the world-famous ten-yearly passion play inaugurated in the plague year of 1633 and still performed by local people. James followed the satnav until he located the MirabelHof along Goethestrasse, and parked his car in a bay area opposite the front entrance of the guest house. He got out of the car, mounted three small steps, and was now standing in front of a frosty glass door through which he could glimpse a hallway with much depth to it. He looked above him and felt a sensation of homely satisfaction, glimpsing narrow balconies on either side decorated with baskets of colourful flowers mounted on the rails. He pressed the bell and waited, a little apprehensive but confident that it would all turn up well just as Sophie described. A few moments passed before the door was opened. James was at that precise moment looking round him, taking in the panoramic view of the houses on either side of the street, their orange rooftops and the various biblical illustrations on their walls and facades. He turned round when he heard the door being pulled open, and suddenly he was facing, what his brain quickly decided, was a very beautiful female specimen, who was in turn staring at him with wide open eyes.

The voice that came was full and assertive, but yet with modesty and enchantment, saying the words ' Bitte '.

James hesitated before saying " My name is James Fletcher, I believe there is a reservation for me. "

" Oh, James, please come in, we have been expecting you, you must be Sophie's brother-in-law ! " said the charming voice. " I am Ursula ".

James did not take his eyes off his German host. He was aware of such an enchanting smile, and attractive blue eyes, and more importantly of a sensation of being at ease, trusting, relaxed and ceding his will entirely to this beautiful girl, to take charge of the situation as she pleases. He followed her into the hallway which led to a long corridor, but halfway down she ushered him to the left into a small office. She went behind the counter, opened a large diary book and asked James to register his name and his UK address. James enquired whether he needed to make any payments at this time but Ursula said

" No rush James, is it alright if I call you James instead of Mr Fletcher, we do not stand on ceremony here. Actually both my parents prefer to be formal with strangers, but I don't. Modern Germany is totally different from the old rigid formal structure, the young are in control, we live and enjoy and do away with social barriers. Sorry I chatter a lot. There is no rush with settling your account, we can do it when you come to leave. How is Sophie by the way ? "

James was impressed with Ursula's mastery of the English language, for he hardly detected any accent, and thought her command of the vocabulary and phraseology matched those of

English natives. Though he wanted to make some comment, he thought it otherwise, that perhaps it was a little premature to be on familiar terms. He knew deep down that he would get to know much more about Ursula during his stay. And yet, his mind was beginning to compare this buxom blonde girl with shoulder length hair, wide shoulders and tall legs, with Christiana, the slender, vulnerable looking girl with chestnut hair and dainty hands. He was not sure why he was making the comparison, why he had this feeling of wanting to lose control of his being, and letting his soul being guided and moulded as Ursula wished, in her own way and her own desire. He was here to find a way out of his pain and his troubled heart, and the only way, he thought, was to let it be, as it comes, as it is suggested by his German host, and whichever way the wind blows.

Suddenly James woke from his reverie when he heard Ursula say
" I will show you into your room which is on the upper floor. There is one other room taken at present, an Austrian elderly couple, whom you will see at meal times, that is breakfast and supper. They are here for Alpine hikes. They come every year. You can bring in your luggage and then we can go up ".
James retraced his steps out of the building, and collected his suitcase from the boot of the car.

" Is it alright to park the car opposite your Hoff ? " said James as he came in again, closing the glass door behind him.

" It is perfectly alright ", replied Ursula, " as you can see, it is a very small town, or a large village rather, and we have none of the traffic restrictions and complications you will find in larger towns and cities ".

Ursula led the way up the staircase, and motioned James to a large double room, modernly furnished, and which had french doors leading to a little balcony that can just accommodate a couple of small chairs, which overlooked the front street.

" I shall leave you, James, to unpack and rest perhaps a little after your journey. Breakfast is served from 7 am to 9 am, and supper is at 7 pm. Please let me know if you need anything, it is very informal here. We are here to make your stay as pleasant as can be. I shall inform my parents of your arrival. See you later James. "

James unpacked, put everything neatly away in the various compartments and drawers of a large modern looking wardrobe, and lay down on the bed after taking off his shoes. He lay on his back, staring first at the ceiling and a little chandelier in crystal glass, which he took for Austrian crystal. Then he looked round him, right and left, taking in the room furniture one by one, first the small desk on his left with its Louis XV style upright chair, stacked against the wall, to the left of the shutters opening onto the balcony, and then the wardrobe he had just used, and to its left the door to the bathroom. The double bed was quite large and James decided it was a Queen's size bed. There was a bed table on either side, each with one drawer. Various pamphlets and magazines lay nicely arranged on all the surfaces.

James closed his eyes. He was in need of rest, not the physical rest for he was hardly tired after his travel, but the mental rest he was looking for, now that he was away from everything that would remind him of the past, of the pain, and of his broken heart. He hoped he would be able to lose himself in his surroundings, the beautiful nature all around, and in trying to discover new places and let himself be charmed by new experiences and new horizons. But he had already been charmed by Ursula, he reminded himself, though the encounter was brief and business like, and he went in his mind over his arrival and his meeting with Ursula again. James could not help feeling drawn to this girl, this place, and to this new experience. He thought to himself that this was a fleeting feeling for he bore much trauma within his heart, and that the presence of Ursula had just hit a raw spot. And yet, he could not stop retracing everything, and in particular Ursula's looks and character. He could see her in his mind, this big blonde girl, the blonde hair down to her shoulders, the bosomy chest, the tall legs and well formed thighs, the wide shoulders, and the full arms. He could recollect her blue eyes, the friendly but staring look, how talkative she was, and how enchanting and radiant she appeared. Suddenly, James felt sad, remembering the love of his life snatched from him, the sadness he has not been able to shake off, not a passing sadness, and not the severe sadness that brought tears to his eyes during the earlier weeks, but a sadness that is halfway, powerful enough to make him stop in his tracks and on the verge of betraying his emotions, and at the same time able to come through the emotion with a lingering light melancholy. He hoped he would be cured, but knew he must not resist if this were to be achieved.

James looked at his watch. It was 6.45 pm. He must have fallen asleep, he concluded, but it was now time for supper. He got up, went to the bathroom, washed his face, after arranging his toiletries on the extended surface beside the washbasin, put deodorant on and rubbed his face with some after shave. He changed his shirt, and headed downstairs for supper as it was now 7 pm.

When James entered the dining room, he met with Ursula's eyes, who was clearly waiting for him to make an appearance. She was in a totally different attire from earlier on, and had changed from working trousers and a blouse to an attractive blue dress and dainty low black shoes. She had taken extra care to put gentle make-up on, and her neck was adorned with a pearl necklace. Herr and Frau Fiege, Ursula's parents, both in their sixties, suddenly appeared, and came forward to greet

James. They enquired whether he found his room comfortable, and hoped he would find the town and the region to his liking. James expressed his gratitude and assured them he was well looked after, throwing a side glance at Ursula. He was ushered to sit down, and found beside him and opposite him Frau and Herr Stauber respectively, the Austrian couple staying at the Hoff, who looked in their fifties. The supper was animated in conversation between the three of them, and from time to time included Ursula, who was busy to and fro looking after her guests. It was a three course menu, and James ate heartily all three dishes, feeling relaxed and at ease with himself and with everything. After the meal, Herr and Frau Stauber invited James to go for a walk with them through the town, which they did every evening, and James had no hesitation in joining them. He would have liked Ursula to also come along, but he understood she needed to stay behind to oversee the Hoff and to make all necessary preparations for the next day. The walk took them through many of the central streets of Oberammergau, and onto the square where the world famous Passion Play is enacted every ten years. Statues and monuments could be seen here and there and in the central square, and a variety of paintings on the fronts of many houses, depicting the life of Jesus. James enjoyed the walk about, and felt invigorated and recharged by the time they returned to the Hoff. Ursula was not around, and James felt a little twang in his heart. He sat for a while in his balcony, and when it had turned quite dark, he closed the shutters, changed into his pyjamas and climbed into bed. He was soon fast asleep.

****

When James woke up the next morning, the first thing he did was to look at his watch he had placed on the bed table. It was

eight. He had slept well, and felt well rested. He had dreamt so
many dreams, he knew that, but as always he could not
remember a single one of them. He was now looking forward to
the day, to seeing Ursula, to going out and exploring that
beautiful part of Bavaria. He thought of Ursula, the number of
times they would come across each other during the next few
weeks, and he hoped he would get to spend a few moments
with her each time. He did not feel confused that he should be
wanting to see Ursula or be with her. Deep down he felt in need
of such friendship, such distraction, and that his whole being
was at this very moment in time longing for such a being to
restore his sanity and his faith in life and in providence. Once
ready he went downstairs. Ursula was there, dressed in
another working outfit, talking to the Austrian couple. James
was greeted by 'Guten Morgen' and he replied the same. He
sat down and helped himself to the coffee jug, and served
himself cheese and ham from the platter on the table. He
looked round to where Ursula was and their eyes met. She was
glancing at him, unaware that he would suddenly turn her way,
and she blushed as they looked at each other. After breakfast,
James lurked around in the lobby. When he saw that Ursula
was finally free and had come to the counter, he approached
her and said
" I was just wondering if perhaps you could give me some
information on where to go or what to visit. "

" Oh, there is so much to see round here and beyond, " replied
Ursula, " and as you are staying for a few weeks, you can
explore at your leisure with no rush, this way you can enjoy
nature fully and at the same time visit palaces and places of art.
"

James hesitated, not knowing what to say next.
Ursula looked at this man in front of her, whom she found
attractive, but there was something else that touched her about
James, something she could not describe to herself, but which

she knew it was no ordinary thing. There was silence for several seconds, which felt to both of them like stillness of time, before Ursula took up the thread of conversation and said

" Actually, I have not much to do in the morning, as the cleaner takes care of the place, and my parents stay in anyway. I could come to show you, a kind of introduction today, and then you will have a good idea of this region and what to do with your time. "

James's eyes lit up and shone, and his face and his smile betrayed extreme happiness, which did not escape Ursula.

" Give me a few minutes to tidy things up, and to change into more comfortable shoes in case we need to walk in the country.
"

A few minutes later, Ursula re-appeared wearing emerald green trousers and a cream blouse, with a scarf round her neck that had flowery designs in a variety of colours. James stood motionless, in awe of the transformation. He thought Ursula looked even more beautiful. They made their way out of the Hoff, and Ursula climbed in the passenger seat. James drove out of town without saying a word, still in awe, and could feel some stirring in his chest, like butterflies hopping here and there where his heart was. Ursula was all the time looking sideways to him. James finally said " Which way are we heading ? "

" Turn right at the next intersection now that we are out of Oberammergau, and then take the second left. We should be taking the Romantische Strasse.

It hit James in a flash as he heard this, and looked at Ursula, gazing into her blue eyes, trying to fathom what it all meant. He knew he had heard the word Romantic in German, and he

knew what the German word Strasse meant. Ursula laughed and said
" Have you not heard of the Romantische Strasse ?
James shook his head.
" Well, this is a very long road that runs parallel to the mountains you see, stretching from east to west. It has always been known by that name, I guess, the old folks must have found it very romantic before our modern times. Till now, couples take this road on a journey of romantic love or to renew their vows. Many a happy ending has come out of driving through this road. "

James was now in total awe, he sensed his being turned upside down, he did not know where his life was heading or what should become of him after his few-week-stay. He looked all around him. It was a mixture of green, blue and white. The green valleys were simply inviting, full of life, radiating peace and tranquility, and then the blue sky above, extending that serenity and that peace, offering hope and contentment in its vast expanse, and finally the snow capping the tall rocky Bavarian Alps with variable peaks and craggy crevices, the sign of the ultimate beauty and the limitless heavenly horizon. He wanted to stop to gaze into Ursula's eyes, hold her hand and say to her how grateful he was feeling at this precise moment, for she had restored to him his inner peace and the ability to see beauty, hope, happiness once more, that he had lost with the passing away of his beloved Christiana.

Ursula took James to Linderhof Palace, which was only a short distance drive west of Oberammergau. She explained to him that it was King Ludwig the second of Bavaria's favourite castle and the embodiment of his baroque fantasies. They visited the palace, and James admired the opulence inside and outside inspired by Versailles. They wandered in the carefully tailored landscape of pond and park, and at the summit of the terraced gardens James admired the palace from afar, the beautiful central fountain and the surrounding ornaments and statues. They stopped in the cafe for coffee and a light lunch. They chatted about King Ludwig's turbulent life and his unexpected and mysterious drowning in Starnberger Lake.

Driving back, James suggested they stop somewhere at the foot of the mountains and stroll in the valley. They found a beauty spot where some cars were parked, empty, their passengers having had in all likely the same idea. The sun was beginning to move down over the horizon, the time when nature is at its most beautiful. James stood admiring the infinite beauty in front of him, then he said to his companion
" Let's venture in ".

Ursula put her left arm into James's right arm and they both stepped into the vast, emerald-green valley. James was aware of Ursula's proximity to him, her body touching his body, her arm rubbing his arm, as they moved forward, and he felt as they advanced into the beautiful nature, a happiness he had long lost and which he thought he would never recover. He felt relaxed, enchanted, in himself and in his surroundings, and most of all, at ease with his companion. His heart was opening up, now ready once more to feel, to share and to experience love. Ursula's mind was dwelling on her life, a life of devotion to her family and to the family's business, and how she had, until this day, never really felt a need to open up, to indulge her heart, to allow intimacy and closeness, and she was enjoying the moment, this new emotion of wanting to be so close, and to wish reciprocity of the same.

They reached a plateau of verdure where they spotted a mound of vegetation that formed a kind of natural settee. They sat down, Ursula still holding onto her man. Instinctively they both turned to face each other, and they gazed into each other's eyes, a gaze that said it all, that expressed the mutual admiration, the desire to spend time together and be together, the tender emotion they were both feeling for each other, an expression of submission and of understanding. Their lips met, in a long kiss, which stirred their core, and they hugged in a fulfilling embrace, holding each other tight, and expressing physically through that unification emotions of love, fulfilment, devotion and hope.

They recovered from their embrace, collecting their thoughts, and sat gazing ahead, squeezing tightly against each other. James put his right arm round Ursula's waist, and she in turn rested her head on his right shoulder. After several moments it was James who spoke first
" Ursula, I need to tell you about my life, and perhaps why I needed to travel abroad for a break. "
" You do not have to tell me anything, our life starts now, what went before concerns you. I am so happy we met. It is a new emotion for me, and I never thought it could come like this, out of the blue, a total stranger I have just laid eyes on him yesterday for the first time. "
Ursula smiled and turned her head slightly to look at James.

" Ursula, it is important for me to tell you. I feel somehow like I am making an important transition, crossing a bridge so to speak, drawn forward while half of me lingering still on the other side of a deep gorge, and I want to move forward, move to be with you, and if I don't tell you, then I shall continue to feel that hindrance, and as much as I want to be with you, I must first remove the shackles that restrict me. "

" Is someone in your life ? Are you married ? ' said Ursula, her face looking grave and somewhat solemn, and suddenly moving her head away from James's shoulder.

" Not at all ", came James's swift reply, " I am not married, there is no one in my life, but there was "

' Oh ", said ursula, " these things happen, and you do not have to tell me. "

" Ursula ", began James but hesitated, clearly betraying his emotions, but after a few moments during which Ursula could see that he was trying to subdue some distress within himself, said

" It had taken me a long time to find true love. I had not loved before, but when I met Christiana, that's her name, I knew it was her. We adored each other, we were head over heels, and we planned it all, our life together, she moving from Copenhagen where she lived, to London. "
James stopped, to take deep breaths, and it did not escape Ursula the faltering voice and the moist eyes.
" I loved Christiana with all my heart, but our love for each other was not meant to continue, not on this earth anyway. She died a year ago. "

James stopped, for he could not go on any further, he knew his being was still raw and suffering.
Ursula turned round to face James, and had to twist herself on that settee-like vegetation, and she put both arms round James's neck, looking at him, as she felt she needed to comfort him, and the fingers of her right hand were fidgeting with James's hair, pulling him to herself, until he rested his chin on her right shoulder.

' I am sorry Ursula, I had to tell you. I came here to forget, but I found you instead, and I am drawn to you, not as a solace, as a temporary keep me sane for a couple of weeks to get better scenario, but actually as a new life, a new love, a new companion, a new hope, and a new beginning, sharing and immersing myself, holding onto a gem, a different gem, not the one I have lost, but a new shining gem that I shall cherish. Providence has taken from me and has given me again, a worthy exchange, and I am only sorry in case you should feel that you came in a subsequent phase of my life. "

" I should only be sorry if your love for me, quickly born, should have been because of your vulnerable heart and nothing more. "

" Oh no, no Ursula. I knew yesterday when I first met you, because I was already making the comparison, and I wanted to be with you. "

" James ", said Ursula, holding onto her man with all her emotional might, " I have also fallen in love, and no matter what the past is I want to be with you. "

Their lips met for the second time.

" I must also tell you about my past " said Ursula, " It is nothing exciting, except that I once knew a man whom I thought I loved. We were together for a few months, but I discovered we were different on almost all fronts, and we parted. He was from Oberammergau, the usual encounter in any village life, I was too young at the time, and I decided then that I should devote my life to helping my parents run the Hoff, and hoping without real hope that may be one day my path should cross my prince charming. And guess what James, it seems to have happened. "

They could now both feel a consuming love, the kind of absolute love that makes the body shivers and the mind overwhelmed, and they could feel respectively their heart fluttering and their sensations aroused. And as they embraced and kissed passionately, Ursula lowered herself on the vegetation and James followed her, and they were united in body and soul, in ecstasy and love, a full union, the man and woman's physical compatibility, the yielding of oneself to the other, the manifestation of love's fulfilment.

Their physical encounter lasted like an eternity before they realised it was time to get back. They walked back to the car, and James drove once again along the Romantische Strasse, this time in the direction of Oberammergau and the Hoff.

James spent a romantic few weeks , and Ursula took him to various places in Bavaria. James was enchanted by Neuschwanstein Castle of King Ludwig II, set in the midst of a forest of fir and pine. He enjoyed most of all travelling along the Romantic Street which stretches across Bavaria, every time they ventured out to visit one place or another. James and Ursula were in complete harmony, and James realised for the first time in a year that he was now ready to move on if he had not already done so. On the eve of his departure, they went out to celebrate their new life together, and Ursula wore a typical Bavarian folk costume outfit, a muslin embroidered pink top with a lavender fitted bodice and a full gathered pistachio free skirt. James saw her radiant and of extreme beauty. They dined on delicious pork roast accompanied by a large potato dumpling and sweet and sour red cabbage over a bottle of dry white Wurzburg wine.

James returned to London, and at the end of his first week back at work, drove to Hereford to see his brother. He broke the good news to them, and Sophie and John were delighted at this prospect, and to see James looking happy and cheerful. James announced that he had decided to quit his job and move to Bavaria to be with Ursula. As Herr and Frau Fiege have been finding it difficult to cope with business on their own, they were hoping for Ursula to take over the management of the Hoff. They also needed a good accountant as with the projected expansion of their business, purchasing and annexing the building next door, and opening a restaurant as well, they would not be able to totally manage everything. They found in James a worthy and trusted man, and moreover their daughter was in love with him, and both were planning to get married not into the too distant future. John was sorry to hear that James would not be living in the same country, but he was aware what this move meant for James. Sophie was whole-heartedly for this new life and adventure, and they both promised they would be visiting James and Ursula to spend a family holiday with them. James tendered his resignation at the London office which was received with some regret. Few weeks later he was installed in the Hoff in Oberammergau, not as a guest this time but as a partner in the business - he was injecting his own funds - and as a companion and a future husband to Ursula.

Life rolled by, and happiness seemed to smile back on James. Ursula never regretted her choice of a man, she found in James the perfect companion, loving and attentive. James felt content, satisfied, in love, and settled resolutely into his new career and status.

Ursula and James married the following spring, the Bavarian life suited him well, he became popular in the village, the business was thriving which pleased Mr and Mrs Fiege, and Ursula cherished her husband with a love bordering on the adoration. In due time they had twin daughters which they named Annabel and Gertrude.

****

THE ARTIST

I wandered along The Strand in London on a sunny Saturday morning, enjoying the walk, and taking in the array of cafes and restaurants that dotted the wide boulevard. I like going to the Strand, it has a special feel about it for everyone, and I think it is because historically it was always popular with the British upper classes right up to the eighteenth century, where you could find important mansions such as Somerset House and Savoy Palace. I normally started my walk from Trafalgar Square going eastwards towards Temple Bar where The Strand becomes Fleet Street. When the aristocracy moved to the West End over the seventieth century, The Strand became well known for coffee shops, restaurants and taverns. During the nineteenth century it was a centre point for theatre, and several music venues still remain to this day. Charles Dickens lived on the Strand.

I decided to go to the Courtauld Museum in Somerset House. I liked to see from time to time the collection they have for Cezanne, one of my favourite painters. As I made my way in through the gate and about to turn right into the small museum, a small board sign caught my attention. It advertised a collection by a contemporary artist in the foyer of Somerset House across from the large central courtyard with fountain. I stopped to read it and noticed that the artist's name was Julie Fenwick. I always find it interesting to see work by contemporary painters, who are not yet well known, and who perhaps are still amateurs and have another profession to help them earn their living, but hoping their artwork would one day be appreciated, and they would be able to break into the art world, and be recognised as an artist of much worth in their own right. I spent about an hour in The Courtauld, satiated myself with Cezanne's paintings, stopped at the basement cafe for a cup of tea and a scone with jam and clotted cream, before making my way an hour later to see Ms Fenwick's work on display in the main house.

On entering the large hall I was struck by several large canvas displayed on tall easels. I counted eight paintings altogether. What struck me the most was the bright and diverse colours of the canvas; scarlet red, deep blue, dark brown, forceful green, and many other colours around those four, and you had to look carefully and with much concentration to discern the actual shapes and objects in the painting. It was as if a prodigy child had done the painting. The colours tired your eyes, but at the same time they drew you in. To me it felt like it was all about the universe, the celestial bodies and the firmament, with the exception of one painting which represented a mast boat being tossed about on the rough seas in a hopeless situation, doomed and losing its battle in the raging storm. Moreover the artist painted the clouds very low and closing in on the sea and the high waves, with no horizon whatsoever, something I had not seen before. As such the painting lacked depth, it was a small stretch of the waters, the boat in its midst, behind it the clouds were closing on it and preventing any escape , and the boat itself tilted and looked about to capsize. Why did the artist paint it like that, I was beginning to wonder, and why did they project it in such a narrow view, the thoughts flitting through my mind. In the other canvas, all I saw was batches of striking colours, many of them scattered in abundance across, and the impression they all imparted was of outer space, of time, and possibly the paradox of creation and fate.

A waiter was circulating among the guests offering light refreshments. The atmosphere was that of an art gallery hired for the sake of an artist wanting to display their work to the public. I looked around trying to spot the artist in question, and opposite one particular canvas I saw a group of people huddled round a central figure, all looking at the painting and listening attentively. As I was not able to see the person doing the talking, I approached and stood behind the group to listen and to get a glimpse of presumably the artist. There were few comments made from members of the public, and when they eventually all dispersed, I found myself standing face to face with a young lady, a brunette, shorter in stature than most, with brown eyes and chestnut hair, and a beautiful looking fair face that had small cute features. Her dress sense matched her paintings, for she seemed to like bright colours, and as I scanned her outfit of blouse, top jacket and skirt, I was again struck by the combination of prints and colours in much variety and along many shades.

' Hello ' I said.
' Hello ' came the reply.
' I find your paintings quite fascinating. '
' Thank you '.
' Obviously it is probably more of modern art than along classic lines. "
' That's right. I want to combine dreams with reality. '
' You mean fantasy world. '
' If you like, but not exactly. We live in a fast changing world where a thought that was once thought of only as fantasy becomes one day a reality. '
' I like the theme. But the shipwreck painting does not fit into your theme of things, we have now modern ships that can sail the seven seas without as much as a flicker of a problem. '

Suddenly the artificial smile she had managed to keep disappeared, and she seemed not happy with my analysis.

' I think I am entitled to paint something different from time to time. '
' But why the gloom ? '
'That's life isn't it ? '
' Absolutely. But there is so much doom and gloom in that painting with no hope of any escape from the storm. That must be the reality side with no dreams in that painting. '
' If you wish. '

' What strikes me is the multitude of bright and very dark colours in your paintings, powerful contrast, overpowering, but may be at the expense of the form. '

' I do not understand you. Can you please explain what you mean? '

' I note two main representations in your paintings. I shall start with the first, and that is the use of strong colour right across the canvas in a quasi haphazard way or so it appears, and one needs to look carefully to perceive the object of the painting. "

' Really ? Do you think so? '

'For me it is. All I can discern is space, the universe, likely the flow of time, but nothing else. The figures which may represent people or particular objects are vague and lost amidst the bright or dark colours that overlap all over. '

' Are you talking about this painting in front of us ? '

' Yes, for instance. I can only see celestial bodies, the universe at large, and yet, which is my second point, there is this very precise geometrical shape which looks like a huge snake permeating the whole painting from one end to the other and which likely represents the direction of time or something along that line. '

' You have a vivid imagination. It is interesting to hear you. A lot of the time I like to know what people make of my paintings, but no one has described it the way you have just done. Actually, it is a fish market, and that's an eel. There are people around the fish carts. '

' Oh, interesting. Which proves my point. The colours are too overpowering to be able to discern anything, unlike the shipwreck in that painting over there. '

' I do not think you appreciate art the way it should be. "

' I do alright, all sorts. It is true I am not too keen on post-modernism, as it can only be understood by the artist, but hardly the public.

She stayed quiet, and looked in discomfiture. And yet I sensed that she wanted me to go on, and for this debate to continue. I thought that she has probably never been challenged before in the way she was now. People visiting art galleries tend to heap praise on anything, but later telling others how strange they thought the art was or how awkward they felt looking at the paintings. To get a good perspective of a new artist you would have to read the critics analysis in the papers.

As I wasn't going to let go I proceeded.
' You are probably familiar with the Golden Section. It is the point at which the onlooker's eye tends to home first, and that is probably where the main thrust of the painting should be. I find in your paintings dispersion to the point of confusion. There should be a kind of linear logic to the painting, like in architecture. Everything in the painting should be directed towards a central point. It is not simply a matter of painterly design. '
' But it is the painter's design. It is the painter's choice of form and colour. We are no longer in the classical age. Modern life has taken over not only in art but in all walks. We dress differently, we work differently, we live differently, and we think differently. I think you are still stuck in the era of classical paintings. '
'Every artist starts their career copying the masters to learn form and technique, don't they ? '
' That is so, but they soon follow the trends of the times. '
' I remember this quote by Luca Paccioli, he was a mathematician who collaborated with Leonardo da Vinci, he said 'Without measurement there can be no art'. '
' What exactly do you want to say ? Do you not like my paintings ? '
' Oh I do, they are attractive at first glance, and many people would hang them in their drawing rooms. Unfortunately now, painting is done under pressure by artists as they need to earn a living, and this speedy painting can only give rise to formlessness, because talented painting is a profession that requires patience and peace of mind. '

' So what is your second point ? '
' These objects you insert in the middle of the multitude of splashed colours look geometrically very well demarcated. If you allow me to observe, and please pardon me, they look like they have been copied and then coloured. '
' I have drawn those, in fact I start with colours straight away. '
' But the lines are very well demarcated and the objects outlines are very well defined ! '
' Is that what you think ? '
' Listen I shall give you a way out, the benefit of the doubt. Your painting compositions, with all their striking colours applied haphazardly, are in fact a form of art dissonance, like what we also find in contemporary classical music. '
And I grinned.

' Hmm. '
' You see, as dissonant your art will be better understood and accepted. But you know as well as I do that superfluous lines and colours can spoil everything, the art itself and its message. Objects don't exist for you, there isn't even a rapport as such between the various parts in any one painting, but it can represent a perpetual revelation. '

Her face lit up, as if she found a life line.
' I think you are beginning to understand my art. It is a continuous revelation, the bringing together of reality and dreams. '

She stared at me for a moment, and I could see the turmoil within her mind, and after a few moments of hesitation said
' I have to go to meet the others. It was nice talking to you. '

She made a hurried escape, going as far from where we were standing as possible, and I thought to myself she must have decided to make her escape at this particular point in our discussion when she thought she had regained some initiative.

The artist never looked in my direction again throughout the evening, and after going round the eight paintings again studying them in some detail I left the hall.

****

KING LEAR OF THE STEPPES

Based on novella by Ivan Turgenev
Lyrics by Nabil Louis

MAIN *CHARACTERS*

MARTIN HARLOV Protagonist, in his sixties, large gigantic figure (big body, broad shoulders, short neck), fair, bushy eyebrows, strong deep voice, talks with grandeur, wears long coat tied with belt, boots

ANNA Harlov's eldest daughter, pretty, attractive, slim, of medium height, wears kerchief, 22 years old

LAMPIA Harlov's youngest daughter, very beautiful, tall, voluptuous, 20 years old

SLOTKIN Anna's husband and harlot's son-in-law, handsome, tall, with curly hair, gun strapped to shoulders most of the time, wears typical Russian costume, 30 years old

ZHITKOV Retired army major, in uniform, Lampia's fiance, looks beaten and broken, 30 years old

BICHKOV Harlov's brother-in-law, displays anger and resentment, wears sporty gear, 40 years old.

NATALIA Harlov's neighbour, in her sixties, conservative clothes.

MAXIMBA Harlov's runner, short stature, Russian peasant costume.

Priest, 2 Officials, Butler, Maids, Peasants, 4 Friends

PROLOGUE

Four friends gathered in a large drawing room of an urban house near Moscow. Through the window, snow flakes are falling. All four are huddled round the fireplace, drink in hand, chatting away.

1st: I'd say no-one is like Shakespeare
    In types he gave no-one came near

2nd: I share your marvel, how it's true
    In life, in norms, in human view

3rd: You name it friends, I've seen them through
    Hamlet, Othello, Falstaff, a few

4th: (*Host saying solemnly*) But gentlemen, I have known a King Lear

1st, 2nd, 3rd: How so?

Host: Just so, in flesh and blood, just so real
    Would you like me to tell you the story?

1st, 2nd, 3rd: Please, please

ACT I

Scene I
Outside his house, Harlov walks surrounded by peasants (minimum 8, male and female) who sing his praises, some of them showing a little snigger

Peasants: How great you are, how strong, a hero
            We worship you, we revere your ego
            You are mighty, your hand is blessed
            The forest bears have known and guessed
            They'll be done with at the very best

Harlov: Ha Ha, will be done with at the very best
It's God's will that my right hand is blessed

Peasants: The thieving peasant among the bees
With cart and horse, master Harlov seized
Over the fence he has thrown with ease

Harlov: Ha Ha, thrown with ease, for I am the best
It's God's will that my right hand is blessed

My family roots way up in 'Schweden'
My grandpa Harlus in Ivan's reign
Came to Russia, drove a troika,
One day announced with a polka,
That he was now a nobleman.
You see that's why my hair is bright
My eyes are blue, my skin is light.

Peasants: Is it true, master Harlov, is it true?

Harlov: If I say it's true then it is true.

Peasant (*woman*): Master Harlov, how kind you are
Like you indeed we've seen nowhere

All peasants repeat above
Master Harlov, how kind you are
Like you indeed we've seen nowhere

Harlov: My dear, for us, lords and masters
We put aside esteem and lustres
That no peasant think of me badly
I will to help in any way gladly
How else can I be a man of honour
My family line stretches way up hither
For I'm mighty, what can they do to me
Where is on earth who can outgun me
(chuckles loudly)

Scene 2

In the house of next door neighbour Natalia; she has a visitor

Natalia: I can hear my dear neighbour Harlov
        Did you know that I owe him my life

Lady Visitor: Tell me about it

Natalia: 'tis long time now, may be 25 years
        My carriage slipped to the edge of a ravine
        The horses had fallen, I was choking with tears,
        As the harnesses snapped, I knew I would be dead,
        When Harlov suddenly appears on the rock,
        My carriage and its wheels he holds and pulls back,
        He saved my life indeed.

        I found him a wife, he was past forty,
        She was seventeen, died soon from frailty,
        Bore him two daughters, Anna and Lampia.

Lady Visitor: I should like to meet this gentleman

(Harlov is shown in by butler)

Butler: Master Harlov

Harlov *(in his usual excited mood)*
        Good day my lady, Natalia, my benefactress. *(he bows to Natalia, then to the other lady; Natalia dismisses with hand the compliment)*

Lady Visitor: I've heard so much about you, Martin Harlov.

Harlov: Natalia is always kind to me
        Yet how can people not fail to notice me

        My grandpa is Harlus the swede,
        A nobleman I am around here,
        800 acres, two lovely daughters

and a runner named Maximba.
Mind you my lady, I am a good boss,
Peasants and serfs praise my good self,
Priests I don't take to,
Church I don't go to,
Only snag is my late wife's brother Bichkof,
A wretched fellow, a sponger in short.

Ladies *(together)* : God bless you Martin Harlov

Harlov: Lady Natalia, please pay me a visit soon.

(Harlov bows and exits)

Scene 3

Harlov's house, in his study, on wall 2 whips, a single-barrelled gun, a sword, horse-collar with brasses, tricorn hat and several pictures; a desk, a sofa, several chairs, lamp stand, large standing clock, chandelier, old piano.

Harlov *(shouting)* : What's up with you, didn't you hear what I said?

Anna: It is ready father, come along.

(Anna lays meal on desk, a plate of rice pudding and a mug of tea. Harlov sits behind desk to eat)

Harlov: Anna, play something on the piano.

Anna: What shall I play?

Harlov: What did they teach you in your boarding school?

(Harlov looks menacingly at her, she plays, he carries on eating, he goes to the sofa and naps, Anna still unaware continues to play first a sad adagio tune then puts in a prestissimo with vengeance, looks round, Harlov does not stir, she covers him and dims the light and exits)

(Slotkin enters, stamping as he walks, holding a shot duck. He wears typical Russian costume with gun strapped to shoulder. Harlov wakes up, muttering under his breath)

Harlov: Why do you always pester me, Slotkin?

Slotkin: I shoot a duck, that will sing for your supper,
I do all the work, you are like my father,
But I'm no better than Maximba your runner.
Martin Harlov, you ill treat the lot of us,
There's never reward but anger upon us.

Harlov: My word is sacred

Slotkin: That's all we hear

(Lampia enters, holding a bunch of flowers, accompanied by Zhitkof in uniform of army major)

Lampia: Father I've picked the best flowers for you
(she looks flirtatiously at Slotkin)
Do you never tire of whining?
Poor Anna with a husband so exacting.
(she arranges the flowers)

Harlov: *(to himself)* She's wilful, she's got cossack blood.

Slotkin: Come Lampia, you know you have the advantage
Over your father, power and bondage,
A good little horse is all I need
If not for me, for Anna your breed.

Zhitkov:
(to Lampia) Sweetheart, my sweet fiancee
(to Harlov) All your problems I will solve,
I've gor understanding and resolve,
Kept a whole army in order,
Won't you make me your governor?

(aloud, while bowing to Harlov): Command ! I will obey *(then rushes to Lampia, kisses her hand)*
        Let me marry your daughter

(Anna returns to the study, stands next to Slotkin, holding hands. Bichkof also enters)

Bichkof: My dear brother, why did you kill off my sister?

(All voicing at once the same lines: Bichkof as above, Slotkin ' Let me marry your daughter ', while Lampia sings ' best flowers for you ' and Anna ' Father, father ', all displaying their different emotions.)

Harlov *(irritated)*: Out of my sight.

(When eventually all leave, to himself): Everything will be alright

(then to Maximba): Maximba, go fetch Lady Natalia at once.

(Harlov is left alone, pensive, restless, in sombre mood)

Scene 4 *(still in Harlov's study)*

(Natalia is shown in by Maximba)

Harlov: How good of you to come *(he kisses her hand)*

Natalia: My dear Martin, you look so sad,
            What's up my friend, is it that bad?

Harlov: Advice I need, I'm going mad

Natalia: Speak, man, speak, I should only be glad
            Doom and gloom in your voice I dread
            Don't keep it in, out with instead.

Harlov: *(kind of whispering, slowly, in staccato-like)*
            What do you think of death?

Natalia: Of what?

Harlov: Of Death,
Can it spare anyone on earth?

Natalia: Have you gone soft in the head?
What will you be thinking next my friend?
Who of us is immortal?
We shall all be lying one day dead.
You've been born giant, but you'll die as well.

Harlov: Oh I will, I will.
I saw things in a dream,
I lay down after dinner, asleep I fell,
I dreamt a black foal ran into my room,
Baring its teeth, a face from hell,
Tearing a skull, a sign of doom,
A warning about my death, I tell.

Natalia: Sure, you've gone soft in the head,
What will you be saying next my friend?

Harlov: A warning, be prepared, O mortal man,
So here I lay before you my plan,
Not wishing that death takes me unaware,
I've decided to act, to show I care,
In my lifetime, bestow in equal share,
The estate on my daughters, my only clan,
Without delay I must act while I can.

Natalia: *(surprise on her face0*
A good idea, only I don't see the need for hurry.

Harlov: I have decided, it is my wish,
I ask you to be a witness,
To the transfer of my property,
To my beloved Anna and Lampia,
The county court has authorised,
Tomorrow at noon all finalised.

Natalia: But you say you want to have my advice,
Surely you are not giving them all at once,
You must keep something for yourself.

Harlov: Not a thing

Natalia: Where will you live?

Harlov: How do you mean - where?
In my own house.
What sort of change can there be, you think?

Natalia: Are you quite certain about each daughter?
Do you trust your son-in-law and the major?

Harlov: My daughters will feed me, their men are push-over,
I'll have enough drink, food, clothes and foot wear.

Natalia: Anna is proud, Lampia is a wolf.

Harlov: What are you saying?
Are you implying
That my daughters should forget
What they owe me? not a jot,
Go against me, their own father,
They'd be cursed, they wouldn't dare,
Not a chance that kind of plot.

(Harlov starts coughing and wheezing)

Natalia: *(calming him down)*
All right, except I don't see why
You are making the decision now,
When everything they will get alright
After you've gone, Oh what a plight !

Harlov: My dear woman,
High power is at work,
While still among the living

             I decide, I put my mark,
             I only ask forgiveness,
             Death is coming for me, hark !

Natalia: I shall be here the morrow
          (then to herself, after Harlov exits)
          To share in your sorrow,
          No good will come of it,
          On his heart a heavy weight,
          Unhappiness is in the offing,
          Poor Harlov, the world will be laughing.

Scene 5

(Harlov's drawing room. All present: Harlov, Bichlov, Anna & Slotkin, Lampia & Zhitkov, Natalia, 2 court officials, priest, another male witness, few guests)

(Harlov in military uniform with sabre. Anna in green and lilac two-tone dress with yellow ribbon, Lampia in rose dress with pink ribbon. All others dressed to occasion. In the middle a table with papers on it. Maximba and maids serve drinks and refreshments. Light music is heard)

Bichkov *(to a guest)* :	Pomposity, pomposity
Guest 1:	We're full of curiosity
Guest 2 *(to Bichkov):*	What a wonderful night of bliss. Are you getting a share in this?
Bichkov :	No my friend, I lodge that's all.
Guest 1 :	What a joyful merry ball

Slotkin *(to Anna)* :	Oh sweety, you'll soon be rich Life will change, old times we ditch
Lampia *(to Zhitkov):*	Shortly this will be my pitch
Zhitkov *(to Lampia)* : *(crossing himself)*	All goes well without a hitch
Harlov :	Ladies and Gentlemen I have asked you to come here for the following reason

                      I am growing old
                      My powers are failing
                      The hour of death like
                      The tide is closing.
                      Not wishing that death catches me unaware,
                      I've decided to act, to show I care,
                      In my lifetime bestow in equal share
                      On Anna and Lampia, my beloved pair,
                      Estate and all, an act of love so rare,
                      Let us rejoice, let us have fanfare.

                      This act *(Harlov bringing his hand down sharply on the papers lying on the table)*,
                      by me has been drawn,
                      And legally sealed as shown,
                      I had my time as king,
                      Now my daughter's turn to sing.

(The official reads out the terms of the transfer)

The Partitional Act of the Estate of the Artillery Lieutenant and Hereditary Nobleman Martin Petrovich Harlov executed by his own hand in full possession of his faculties makes the following stipulations:
The 800 acres divided equally between Anna and Lampia Harlov.
The stable and farm house go to Anna.
The main house goes to Lampia, the youngest daughter, according to tradition.

(Slotkin holds Anna, trembling all over. Zhitkov licks his lips and glances sideways at Lampia. Anna and Lampia appear ecstatic)

(The official continues)

Martin Harlov gave himself the right to live in the rooms he occupied, full lodging and board, with ten roubles a month.

Harlov *(barging in)* : If they fulfil my will
                     My blessing go with them,
                     But if they don't they will
                     Call down my curse, Amen.

(Anna sinks to her knees and bows her head, her husband Slotkin follows suit)

Harlov *(to Lampia)* : Well, what about you?

(Lampia bends down to the floor, Zhitkov bends his whole body forward)

(Harlov signs, then says to his daughters)

Sign here *(pointing to bottom of paper)*
I thank you and I accept. Anna *(Anna signs)*
I thank you and I accept. Lampia *(Lampia signs)*

(witnesses sign, official fold documents, refreshments and drinks circulate, music, all dance, peasants are seen through window cheering. Harlov sits in armchair in corner, talking to guests, at times pensive. He gets up and heads for the garden)

Scene 6

(In the garden, a group of peasants. Harlov stands a short distance away, listening without being noticed)

Peasant 1 :   Our master's still alive

                        Yet he owns us no more.

        Peasant 2 :   Wonders will never cease
                        What did he do it for?

(Peasants drinking, while Bichkov comes out, talking to a guest)

        Bichkov :   They'll throw him out one day,
                        Just you wait, mark my say,
                        Bloody fool Harlov is,
                        They'll dispose of him outwith,
                        Chuck him out in the snow,
                        Will he not see the blow ?

        Harlov   *(comes forward agitated)*
                        What are you going about?
                        Hold your tongue or suffer a clout *(he raises his arm)*

        Bichkov :   God knows what a real fool you are,
                        You *(pause)* killed off my little sister,
                        As for me a devoted brother,
                        Not a farthing, what do you care !

(Anna, Slotkin, Lampia, Zhitkov, come out on hearing the commotion. Natalia and some guests follow)
        Harlov :   *(to Slotkin first then to Bichkov and the others)*
                        Stop, be quiet, don't poke your nose.
                        If I've decided so it goes.
                        Who can go against my will,
                        I can end it all, right now still,
                        You should all show gratitude.

        Natalia :   Your act today was a great deed.

(Both Anna and Lampia listen emotionless)

        Anna :   Father dear, calm yourself, do not despair,
                        They don't know us, how can they declare,
                        Such hurtful things, such words so unfair,
                        Don't fret yourself, look at your poor face,

Shame on you Bichkov, you're a disgrace.

(Zhitkov nudges Lampia, she does not stir)

Harlov :   Thank you Anna, in you I have trust,
           This good-for-nothing has long been outcast,
           I am off to my room, good night, I must
           Remember I'm not master here now but a guest.

(Harlov departs, Anna and Lampia dance with Slotkin and Zhitkov, all looking happy. Bichkov remains outside watching. Guests slowly filter back into the house)

Bichkov : They'll give him the boot alright.

Natalia : No good will come of it.

CURTAIN

ACT II

Scene 1

(Few weeks later, Natalia's house. Harlow, unkempt, sitting in armchair. Natalia is serving tea.)

Natalia: You are a free man now,
           You must feel a lot happier.
(Harlov lowers his head)
           Do I sense your soul is sad?

                    Are you consumed by regret?
                    Are you dreaming still of death?
                    In the Lord put all your faith.

Harlov: I am suffering deep inside,
(stands up)   My torment I cannot hide,
                    My restless soul would not find
                    The peace I longed for, on my side
                    A trail of evil I have for guide.

                    (Natalia comforting him)

                    Death is coming, I know for sure,
                    I keep a watch, I have no fear,
                    But what is devouring me my friend
                    I never thought like this I'd end,
                    The kin I loved and gave much for,
                    They show no feelings, they care no more,
                    Blocks of stone they have become,
                    A loveless place is my old home,
                    I never thought I would see the day
                    When my daughters would turn this way.
(choking)   They don't even speak, how hard can they be,
                    I've got not long to live, things are bad for me.

Natalia :   You should have listened
                    When you came for advice.

Harlov :   I've always shown Lampia preference,
                    Yes I see no gratitude at all,
                    Her heart is fiery, like a burning coal,
                    I'm her father, she owes me deference.
                    If she turns out an ungrateful child
                    I will kill her with my very own hands.
(Natalia gasps)
                    I'm not the kind to pity myself,
                    I'm not the kind to lose my nerve,
                    But I will not my words renounce,
                    The world will fly very soon to pieces,
                    I don't regret what I have done,

When the crunch comes, I've had my reasons.

(*Harlov leaves slowly, Natalia is left pondering*)

Natalia : It's all wrong, Oh it's all wrong !

Scene 2 (*Harlov's house, Lampia and Zhitkov on stage*)

Zhitkov : Lampia, I love you, please listen, I plea,
That devious Slotkin has played his little tricks,
Don't you see he is driving a wedge between us,
How can Anna allow him the charge of those bricks?
(*he points to the walls*)

Lampia : I never consented to your marriage proposal,
So take my advice and leave this house,
For it will always be No, I will not be your prize.

(*Zhitkov leaves looking sad, Lampia observes herself in a wall mirror, few moments later Slotkin and Anna enter*)

Slotkin : These peasants need clipping round the ear,
They work little, they have no care or fear.

Anna : I do agree my darling,
The harvest is nearly here,
I sent away the weak
And those who are not dear,
The rest will have to work as hard,
Or out they go, I made it clear.

Slotkin : You've got to bash them, instil the fear.

Anna : (*after a pause*)
Tell me, why did you sell father's horse?

Slotkin : Like we agreed I did of course,
Simply eating hay for nothing,

             Now it's helping with the ploughing.

(Harlov enters, unshaven, dressed in tatters, despondent and very depressed)

Slotkin : Look at him;
 He has fallen into his second childhood.

Harlov : Anna, Lampia *(looking round him at them, imploring)*

Slotkin : We cannot do all the eccentric things he wants.

Anna : We should show him respect and wont.

Slotkin : Do we Anna ?

Anna : You have sent away Maximba.

Slotkin : Young and stupid, thick and artless,
 He's gone to learn to make a harness,
 This way at least he'll earn his keep.

 (approaching Harlov, pointing to him)

 He has clothes and shoes,
 He has food to eat,
 If we don't give him money,
 It's because we don't have it,
 We treat him as a parent,
 Sincerely we do,
 Though we need his rooms,
 We try to make do.

 (addressing Harlov directly)

 Oh you do approve of us, don't you?
 Once you were hot-tempered and sharp,
 Now quiet and as soft as a harp.

(Anna takes Harlov in, leaving Lampia and Slotkin on stage. Lampia flirts with Slotkin, he returns her caresses)

Lampia *(singing)*
>Look for it, look for it, thundercloud threatening,
>While father-in-law 'tis I who will be killing !

Slotkin :   The things that get into your head.

Lampia :   What?

Slotkin :   What is it you have just said?

Lampia :   It's a song.
>You know you can't leave words out of a song.

(she cracks a laugh, they embrace)

Scene 3 *(Harlov's study, he sits on a sofa, dishevelled, in tattered clothes, with Anna beside him)*

Anna :   Your robe is torn, your beard not shaven.

Harlov :   It does not matter.

(he gets up)

>When I was a boy
>I respected my father,
>If I messed about
>A whip was the thrasher,
>I endeared him for it,
>He was no real terror,
>His love was deep at heart,
>Same love I passed to my heir,
>I have grown old, what do I get?
>I'm pushed aside, I have no rest,
>I seem to remember I had two daughters
>I put in charge, I was not clever,

>   Gone has my farm, in tip-top shape,
>   Is this my house? Can I escape
>   The torment, the distress, the loss of face,
>   The humiliation by your husband's grace?

(Anna shows anxiety and distress)

>   Do I give in, Do I retreat?
>   Deep in my soul, my sorrow is great. *(Harlov weeps)*

Anna : Father, father.

Harlov : Go away, go away *(faltering voice)*

(Anna runs off, Harlow by himself looking dejected)

(Natalia enters)

Natalia : I think I know everything,
          Heavens, I sense a foreboding.
          My dear Martin, you come with me,
          You have a home, don't let it be,
          That son-in-law with their consent
          Treats you wickedly in all intent.
           You are magnanimous, above par,
           In our time, too rare by far,
           A risk you took when you handed over,
          You threw everything in the water.
          Show your scorn, come with me,
          You deserve better for the life of me.

Harlov: The fear of death ruined my mind,
          I have myself to blame, and to save my pride,
          I didn't say a word, I avoided every soul,
          Now everyone is saying the silly old fool.
          They took my servant boy,
          They cut off my allowance,
          I lost my horse and carriage,
          It's my cross, my penance,
          Shame is now my clothing,

Disgrace and self loathing,
Oh God of mercy, have pity on your slave.
I am staying put, I'll see this to the grave.

(He waves her to go, reluctantly she leaves. Lights dim, he lies down for the night, then sunshine through window, another day)

Scene 4 *(still Harlov's study, Harlov gets up, walks to the table, pours himself a glass of water, looks in the mirror on the wall, scrutinises his face, walks back to the sofa, inspects his clothes. Suddenly Slotkin comes in followed by Lampia)*

Slotkin : Your room is needed to run the farm.

Lampia : You can sleep in the attic.

Harlov : *(to Lampia)*
I can understand Anna being his slave,
She is his wife, she could not be brave,
But you, Lampia, you *(in a chocked voice)*
I shall never forget this, right to my grave,
He has enchanted you, swayed you by his charm,
You've given yourself freely into his arms,
Is that the reason you sent away your soldier,
Turned out your 'uncle' *(mockingly)*, deceived your sister?
And those poor peasants under your oppression,
What's their fate to be, bearing their passion?
Heavens above will be my witness,
A perpetual weight sits on your conscience.

(after a pause, addressing both Lampia and Slotkin)

Every timbre in that house,
I have laid with my own hands,
You throw me ... out *(chocked voice)* ...from
My home, my farm, my land !

(Harlov stretches his body up, looks them in the eye, and walks out. Slotking hunches his shoulders and stretches his arms. Lampia turns her back on him and leaves the room)

Scene 5 *(Natalia's house, Natalia with Bitchkov, the butler announces Harlov)*

Butler : Master Harlov

(Harlov enters, looking still dishevelled, in rags, and in an agitated state)

Harlov : They have thrown me out.

Bichkov : Exactly what I said,
You didn't listen to me then.

Natalia : Don't let it get you down,
You will find home in mine,
Have supper then get some sleep.

(to the butler)
Whatever he wants he gets indeed,
Clean his clothes, shave his beard,
Get the tailor to take his measures.

Butler : Yes ma'am, this way if you please *(to Harlov)*

Natalia : I've never forgotten you once saved my life.

Harlov : Now you are saving ... my .. life.
(slowly)

Natalia : I shall help you, but in future
You promise to listen to me,
And evil thoughts you don't nurture.
Get a wash and a bite,
Lie down for a good sleep,
Tomorrow we'll talk it over,
The pit cannot be that deep.

(Harlov exits with the butler. Natalia and Bichkov are both pensive)

Scene 6 *(a bedroom in Natalia's house. Harlov sitting on the bed edge, still in his tatters, bare feet. Bichkov enters.)*

Bichkov : Harlov the swede, look now on your descendent,
Can you recognise him? Not exactly resplendent.
You used to call me sponger, hanger-on,
Now you have got no home of your own.
We both are in the same boat,
You will be fed on hand-outs,
How high and mighty you were,
How you used to put on air,
You divided your estate,
Did you get that gratitude
You kept on shouting about,
I told the truth when I said,
They'll drive you out bare-backed.

Harlov : *(looking very depressed, suddenly furious)*

Watch out, or you'll be out of a frying pan.

Bichkov : *(with extreme sarcasm)*

Not a rag to your back, and a bully you remain,
Where's your house and your home,
Oh it gives me too much pain
Landowner, nobleman, esquire, they have driven you insane.

Harlov : *(very furious, standing up, agitated like a wild beast)*

House and home !
I will destroy their house and home,
They won't have any, anymore,
Then they'll know I'm Martin Harlov.

(Harlov dashes out of the room)

CURTAIN

ACT III

Harlov's house and courtyard. Harlov on the roof-top, in his tatters, bare-feet, tearing planks and smashing with his fist.

Harlov : They shall not have my house and my home.

In the courtyard, Anna, Lampia, Slotkin, Maximba, other servants and maids. A state of agitation around. Natalia and Bitchkov arrive. Also Zhitkov appears. Slotkin is throwing ropes and nets at Harlov. Anna and Lampia appear to be in a state of shock.

Shouts of : Come down father.
Come down master Harlov.
Hurry, get some help.
Call the authority.

Harlov keeps on smashing roof top, bare framework now beginning to appear in one section. Planks come hurling down, heaps of wood pile up on the ground. Harlov shakes the chimney, which gives way, tearing it down.

The courtyard is full of people. The priest appears, holding a cross, officials arrive, peasants gather. Slotkin gets a gun, aims at Harlov, only to be pushed away by Anna.

Slotkin : He's gone mad, he's gone round the bend,
If I shoot him, the law is on my side,
I've got the right to defend my land,
And I will shoot if you don't come down.

Harlov : Shoot, shoot,
And here is something for you.

(he sends flying a piece of board which lands at Slotkin's feet. Slotkin jumps, Harlov roars with laughter)

(Slotkin seizes Maximba by the scruff of the neck)

Slotkin : Get up there, save my property,
A ladder, fetch a ladder.

Maximba gets a ladder, hooks it up on one side, climbs up half way, tries to persuade Harlov to come down. Other servants do not stir, but keep watching scene, despite Slotkin urging them for help.

Harlov : Is that you, my dear Maximba?

Another part of the roof comes crashing down, Maximba retreats. The house top is reduced to a skeleton. Slotkin takes aim again. Lampia pulls him by the elbow.

Lampia : Don't you dare,
Father is destroying his own house.

Slotkin : It's ours.

Lampia : You say it's ours, I say it's his.

Harlov : *(roaring from above0*

Very good, very good, what about your boyfriend,
Do you not like kissing, are you not having fun?

Lampia : Father

Harlov : Yes daughter

Lampia : Stop father, come down,
We are to blame,
We shall return everything to your name.

Slotkin : What are you giving away all your property for?

Lampia : I'll give back my own part,
Stop father, come down, forgive me.

Anna : Forgive us father.

Harlov : Your strong hearts have been stirred too late,
There is no way out, no stopping fate,
I am not leaving one beam upright,
I shall destroy with all my might,
This house where I have lived for years,
Away from me satans, I don't trust your tears.

Lampia : Enough father, forget the past,
We have sinned, you've seen the last.

Harlov : Fine words, but you've killed my trust,
You're not my daughter, I'm not your father,
I am a man who has been done for,
I shall not take back my gift,
Today I put an end to it.

(Harlov continues to destroy the house, still perched on the roof)

Lampia : Father

Anna : Father, dear father

Harlov continues to hurl down rafters, to shake the beams, when all of a sudden, the whole strutter collapses and Harlov with it. People dash forward, pull a beam off Harlov, lift Harlov and set him on a near-by bench.

Maximba comes up, goes down on his knees and holds Harlov's hand. Lampia stands in front of her father, her eyes fixed on him. Anna comes also close. Slotkin stays back. Natalia approaches.

Harlov opens his eyes, says in a feeble trembling voice

Harlov : There it is, the black foal.
(then looking at Lampia)

It's you I won't forgive.
(Lampia falls at Harlov's feet)

Harlov dies.

Anna stands silent. Slotkin withdraws into a corner, throws his gun. Maximba and other peasants remove head gear and cross themselves.

An old-grey-haired peasant : You did wrong by the old man,
You have a sin on your soul.

All peasants : You did wrong by him, you did wrong by him.

EPILOGUE

In the urban house, near Moscow, the four friends still gathered in the drawing room, drink in hand, around the fireplace. The host continues his story.

Host : Few days after the funeral, Lampia left for good,
She sold her share to Anna, all trace of her was lost,
Anna survived her husband, the rumour she poisoned him,
She lived happily ever after, a landowner in her own right.

And that is the story of King Lear of the Steppes.

(the speaker falls silent)

****

Printed in Poland
by Amazon Fulfillment
Poland Sp. z o.o., Wrocław